To the Black Women
We All Knew

To the Black Women
We All Knew

Kholofelo Maenetsha

Published in 2014 by Modjaji Books
PO Box 385, Athlone, 7760, Cape Town, South Africa
www.modjajibooks.co.za

Edited by Bronwyn McLennan
Cover artwork by Tammy Griffin
Book and cover layout by Andy Thesen

Printed and bound by Megadigital, Cape Town
ISBN 978-1-920590-07-9

For my beloved mother,
Rosemary Annah Maenetsha

Chapter 1

It was a quilt they made: their needles moved in and out of the pieces of fabric they were sewing together to form one intricate pattern. With a jab of her needle, a hole was made, leading Matlakala along a path of patches and colours. Matlakala, meaning rubbish. She had been given this name because she was born after a stillborn baby; this was a way to protect her from her ancestors who might find her worthy, as they had the other child. So her mother devalued her before they could take her away too.

Matlakala's hands moved feverishly over her patchwork, creating zigzags on the cloth. If looked at closely they resembled Egyptian hieroglyphs. In her slightly high-pitched voice, more like that of a child than a woman of twenty-four, Matlakala murmured to herself, as if deciphering the patterns on the cloth.

"If love could speak, it would look deep into my soul and tell me what lies there. If love could speak I believe it would say ... ow!" The sound escaped Matlakala's lips. She put her pricked finger to her mouth, dulling the pain.

"If you stopped day-dreaming, Matlakala, you wouldn't hurt yourself," Pamela said, not looking up from her work. Her needle moved with slow, calculated movements. Pamela, whose plump figure bordered on obese, was the perfect wife to her husband and a doting mother to her children. Maybe it was her extra weight that slowed her movements, or maybe it was her way of meditating. If asked, her needle would meekly say: "Love, for a woman, exists for only an hour. She is bound by dreams, imaginings. Hoping it will last a lifetime. But a lifetime is only wedding cakes and memories of that one day. When she said I do."

A long sigh escaped Pamela's lips as her mind turned to her wedding day. It had been beautiful. Just the thought of that day cheered her, momentarily relieving the pain she was feeling in the present. Pamela's eyes filled with tears at the thought of the wrong turns her marriage was taking. It was a long, unrelenting journey that was not likely to end well. Pamela sniffed. She had to be strong, especially for Ama. This was her day. For the first time since she had started working, Pamela looked up at the bride to be. She felt both pity and joy for her friend. Maybe Thabo, Ama's fiancé, was different. Pamela bent her head, returning to her work and sending a silent prayer to the heavens for Ama.

As though receiving these blessings from above, Ama stretched out one arm and smiled. Although not beautiful, Ama's face was pleasant, with wide eyes and small lips. Her quiet nature irritated some people, like Beauty, who felt that women shouldn't display their weaknesses and rarely tolerated such qualities in anyone. Beauty was the queen bee of the quartet. She brought energy and laughter to every space she entered. Now her needle moved swiftly but carefully through the fabric, her fingers caressing the cloth. Her eyes were bright with the colours she was sewing together and her lips moved slightly, whispering the notes of a tune.

"Beauty, are you ever going to get anywhere with that?" Ama asked, wondering at Beauty's smile. It was the smile of someone in love. For as long as she could remember, Ama had never smiled so sweetly or happily. Even after Thabo had proposed, Ama had never found herself beaming idiotically because of love. The feeling of bliss had eluded her somehow. Although they had never told her, Ama knew that Beauty and her brother Jeffrey were involved, though she hadn't realised until now that their involvement went as deep as Beauty's infuriating smile revealed. Was she truly in love with Thabo Ama wondered. She was going to marry him the day after tomorrow. Ama fixated on Beauty's smile, could I spend the rest of my life with him? It made her feel lost, unsure about what was between her and Thabo. Did she really want to marry him? Surely she should know by now. Ama felt like crying. The half-finished quilt spread out on each woman's lap was being made for her. For a moment she felt like she couldn't breathe. Was it supposed to feel like this, like being trapped?

After a while, Ama said softly, "The cake will be ready for the last viewing tomorrow."

"Isn't tomorrow a bit late?" Beauty said.

"No, it's for any last minute changes I want to make."

"Wow! Everything is happening so fast, isn't it?" Matlakala said, fantasising about weddings and love, until Joe drifted into her mind, and her brows furrowed in pain. She wouldn't think of him now.

"Yes," Ama said, not sure whether to be pleased or not.

"Falling in love is the most beautiful thing," Matlakala said, smiling like a teenage girl with her first crush. At that, Beauty released a disgusted snort. The others turned towards her.

"There's no need to be cynical, Beauty. I believe every woman deserves a man that will love her, that's all."

"Well I guess you would know, Matlakala, wouldn't you? I mean Joe doesn't speak to you, he sleeps with every woman that walks, drinks like a fish …"

"Must you be so mean all the time?" Ama shook her head.

"What? I'm saying what's on my mind and what we all know is the truth. I mean really, if that's what you call love, please spare me. I can do without that kind of love, the love that black women suffer to keep some man in their life, and for what?" Beauty gestured towards Pamela.

Pamela knew that people talked about her, judged her, even. She was a statistic, one of the millions of abused women around the world, a fact she resented. Maybe I should just kill Mandla and go from being the abused to a murderer. Take back my power, Pamela thought.

"I believe your father did wrong by you, Beauty. No woman should be this cynical." Beauty looked at Ama, her emotions chasing after each other across her face. Anger won.

"My father did right by himself. I believe every human being has the right to do right by him- or herself."

"But the question is, did he do right by you?" Ama persisted.

"You know what? I think it's time for me to get going. I'm afraid if I open my mouth right now I might say something I'll regret." In her hurry, Beauty carelessly tossed aside her needlework, tangling threads and brightly coloured cloths. She picked up her bag and began to make for the door.

"Beauty." Ama's voice was gentle.

"What?"

"Jeffrey asked me to tell you to come and see him once we're done here. He's out back."

"You can tell your brother I'll see him tomorrow, like we arranged."

"But Beauty …"

"Ama, Jeffrey and I are fine. Don't worry yourself." She turned and left.

"Some relationships are complicated, aren't they?" said Matlakala.

"I never could tell what my brother saw in her."

"Hush, she's our friend," Pamela said relaxing into her chair. Whenever Beauty was around, ever since they had talked about her situation, she felt a yoke of tension around her shoulders. She felt guilty and helpless for involving her friends in her problems. She'd been married to Mandla for sixteen long years. And her friends had been there for every broken bone and swollen muscle, but people have their limits, and Pamela feared they had reached theirs.

"I know she's our friend and everything, but she's just so …"

"Ama, please don't gossip. It never helps," Pamela said.

"I wasn't going to say anything bad. I just …"

"What, Ama?" said Matlakala.

"I'm scared. In a way, Beauty is right. Why does it seem like loving a man is more about sacrifice than two people coming together because they love each?"

"Do you love Thabo?" Pamela asked.

"Yes, very much."

"Then, there it is."

"Were you afraid, Pamela? Was it as easy as waking up and putting on your shoes?" Ama asked.

Pamela swallowed hard. Had it been easy, marrying Mandla?

"No, it wasn't easy, but not being with him would have made it worse."

Matlakala felt tears prick her eyes. She bent her head so that the others could not see her sadness. She might dream of love in her fantasies, but reality was a different matter.

"So that's why it's hard for you to leave him, even now?" Ama asked, still wanting to appease her own fears.

"Ama, sometimes a woman loses sight of her needs. All she can see is her husband and children. Her life is no longer hers alone."

"The way you love him, would you die for him?" Ama continued.

"I don't know about that," Pamela said, smiling. Ama seemed to understand Pamela's joke because she smiled too.

"Come on back to work, tomorrow is our last day before the big wedding." Pamela feigned excitement. With faith they would make it through, she thought. The three women worked quietly, forgetting time. Their hands turned the hours into a black blanket of night. It was the comforting companionship of being with other women working together that lulled Pamela into forgetfulness. She felt happy and free in that moment. Then it struck her – she was late. She felt a familiar panic rising. It was a fair distance from Meadowlands Zone 9 to Dobsonville.

"I have to go" she said.

"I also need to go." Matlakala got up, gathering her pieces of fabric into a neat pile.

Outside, Matlakala quickly flagged a taxi to Pimville, while Pamela watched anxiously, hoping a taxi going to Dobsonville would come soon. She looked at her watch – quarter to eight. At this hour, taxis were scarce. And she still had to get off at the shopping centre and walk down Elias Motsoaledi, past the police station, to reach home.

"God, please not tonight," Pamela muttered to herself as she walked down Maseru to stand at the T-junction in front of the White Church. Luckily, after a few minutes a taxi stopped to let her on. Maybe she wouldn't be so late after all. But still she could not shake her sense of dread.

As usual, Beauty's house in Zone 5 was dark. Lights were used sparingly by the two inhabitants. It was a house of lingering shadows. Wedged between an unofficial dumping site and Meadowlands Stadium, behind the Lutheran Evangelise Church Mission, it was like God Himself had turned His back on it.

A rustling noise came from behind a door she was passing on her way to her bedroom. Her mother was still awake, probably reading one of her romance novels, oblivious to the late hour.

"Beauty." Mma Maluse had a funny way of singing her name, dragging every syllable until the last.

"Yes, Ma." Beauty could hear her getting out of bed and shuffling towards Beauty's bedroom.

"Put on the light, child," her mother said. "You can't be scared of yourself forever." She flicked on the light as she crossed over to the bed.

"I was about to go to sleep, I didn't see why I should switch on the light when I will switch it off in a minute," she said.

"I wonder, if you looked like me, how you would feel. I sometimes get out my old photos and compare them to what I see in the mirror now. They might as well be two different people. Today I look at myself and I am this mutant version of myself," she said, laughing.

"Stop that, it's not funny."

"No, it's not, but when you look like me you have no option but to laugh at everything, unless you want to cry at your own reflection," she said, sounding a little sad. "Anyway, what happened to you today, why did you come back so late?"

"I was angry, so I went for a walk."

"When will this anger stop, Beauty? You're becoming more like your father, you know."

"Don't compare me to him," Beauty said, getting under the covers.

"And what did you find on this walk of yours?"

"Nothing."

"Not even that boy, what's his name again?" she patted Beauty on the knee.

"Jeffrey."

"Yes him, tell me about him again."

"There's nothing to tell."

"You know what I mean"

"Not tonight, Ma, I'll tell you some other time."

"I'd like to meet him."

"No, Ma, I'm sorry," Beauty said, careful not to hurt her feelings.

"I know, baby, I was just dreaming. Forget I said anything. How are the wedding preparations going?"

"Everything is fine. We're going to view the cake tomorrow."

"You are happy for her, baby, aren't you?"

"Ama? Yes, I am." She was truly happy for her. They had been friends for a long time. The four of them had met in one of those teenage youth programmes that Kliptown was famous for.

"You should be. You must be happy all the time."

"Yes, Ma."

"Do you remember … Never mind." Beauty knew what her mother had wanted to say. She'd wanted to say, do you remember when you were just this big, and I had you in my arms? We twirled around laughing so hard our rib muscles hurt. That was her mother then, back when the world accepted her, before her body had been changed beyond recognition. Now she lived like a monster in a dark house.

"I remember, Ma," Beauty said.

"What are you going to do tomorrow?"

"We're going to finish the quilt, view the cake and we'll be done."

"Ah, the quilt. It's the best gift for a couple: a quilt of the most colourful cloths sewn together with love and care. All that goodness binds the love together. The love will always be strong."

"Ma, love fades no matter what you do."

"Love doesn't fade, baby. It is the way you look at the person that changes. Love remains the same."

Not for the first time, Beauty wondered at her mother's ability to stay so positive. "So," she said, "you want to know about Jeffrey." Beauty shifted closer to her mother, who was sitting on the edge of the bed. "I don't know what happened between us. He's always been there,

Ama's older brother. I never thought much of him, and then one day, something happened. We were all at Orlando Stadium, watching the Soweto Derby. Jeffrey was sitting next to me. The Pirates were winning, and we were ecstatic, jumping up and down. Then he hugged me. And something changed between us." Beauty smiled.

"He's an architect," Mma Maluse said.

"Yes, and he's trying to open up his own business."

"Wow, that's impressive!"

"Go to sleep mother," said Beauty, rolling over, an unbidden smile on her lips.

Matlakala got off the taxi in Pimville, at the robot on Chris Hani Road in front of Maponya Mall. As she walked up Mohwelere Road, she wondered if Joe would be home. But there were no lights on, and the note she had left for him was still pinned to the fridge.

Sighing, she began making dinner. When she was finished, she dished up for two, leaving Joe's plate in the microwave. Sitting at the kitchen table, she eyed the coal stove: the house was unusually cold, even in summer. Maybe she should start a fire. The house would be warm by the time Joe got home. She wished it were as simple to warm the cold that had settled in her life.

Ama had tidied up the house, packing the half-finished quilt and the pieces of cloth into a box. Now she stood at the sink washing the dishes. A couple standing beneath the glow of a streetlight caught her eye. Ama looked at them through the kitchen window, watching as they embraced. She thought of Thabo, and hoped the anxiety she felt about the wedding was just cold feet. It is normal to feel this way, she told herself. There is nothing to worry about. Looking up again, she saw that the couple had gone. She wondered what they might be doing now, whether they had gone their separate ways or if they had gone somewhere together – out for a drink, or home to bed. Letting out the dishwater, she yawned. It was time for sleep.

Chapter 2

Soweto at night: the street lights hang from the night sky, amber bulbs bobbing up and down, illuminating the souls below. But to see the lights this way, you'd have to be somewhere you never thought you'd be, your senses dulled by pain and fear, and the feeling in your chest that you were about to die. Like in the back of Ama's brother's van speeding its way to Chris Hani Baragwanath Hospital, your back pressed hard into the metal floor, your body vibrating with the rhythmic engine.

Pamela lay on the hard metal looking up at the yellow bulbs. In her eyes, they were beautiful and they held a life of their own. They seemed to be watching Pamela on her journey to the hospital. Soon it will be your last, the lights were saying, as they stared at her. Pamela blinked, looking through the streets lights to find the stars. There was always some hope in them, but she could hardly make them out in the glare of the lights. Pamela had lost count of how many times her husband had beaten her. It hardly hurt anymore, not like it had the first few times, before she had begun to feel numb. The reasons for the beatings no longer seemed to matter either. In fact not much seemed to matter any more, except her children.

A tear rolled down Pamela's cheek as she thought about them. They had been awake when she rushed through the door from Ama's house. Now, speeding down to Bara, Mandla's rules drummed in her head.

"No wife of mine comes home after seven!" Mandla had glared at his wristwatch. "I won't have you gallivanting around Soweto doing God knows what. See kids, your mother doesn't love you. She doesn't even want to come home when you're here." Pamela had felt the familiar fear that swept through her body whenever Mandla spoke about love and the lack of it in the house. As she'd helped her children to bed, she'd prayed to God that tonight of all nights he'd let her be.

The van jerked a little, turning her face to the left. The cut on her left cheek came into contact with the warm metal, opening the wound. Blood flowed out, creating patterns on the metal floor. She would probably get stitches, she mused. It always took a few stitches and resetting of bones to get her fixed.

Pamela felt the van slow down. Maybe they were at the gate, she thought. Soon she'd be on a stretcher, then in some examining room. That's if there were no cases more serious than hers. But they were lucky, and in no time she was fixed up. The nurses at the hospital had stopped asking questions. They knew she would be back soon enough.

Pamela came out of casualty in a wheelchair. Her left cheek was stitched, as predicted, and her right arm was in a sling. It wasn't broken this time. Thank God for small mercies, she thought.

Ama and Jeffrey were still waiting at reception. "Hey you two, what are you still doing here? It's late, you should go home. As you can see, I'm fine." She brandished her slung arm. "It's not broken, thank God." She laughed lightly. The whole situation was embarrassing for her.

"Are they going to keep you overnight?" Ama asked. Jeffrey placed his hand on Ama's shoulder.

"We'll see you, Pam," he said, guiding Ama to the exit door.

"By the way, who phoned you?" Pamela called after them. She knew it couldn't have been Mandla.

"It was Sizwe. I think he was scared, but I told him you were fine."

Sixteen years old, Sizwe was Pamela's firstborn. A tear slipped from her eye as she thought of her son seeing her collapsed on the bedroom floor.

A nurse came and pushed her on to the female ward. At least she could get some sleep, and try to forget.

Matlakala had gone home with dreams of love, weddings and cakes. In her happy state she'd wished she'd find it waiting for her when she stepped through the door of her house, in the form of Joe, her sort-of fiancé. But he wasn't there. These days he was hardly ever home. Whatever it was they'd had wasn't there anymore. These days he came and went as he pleased, and every night Matlakala anxiously waited for him, waited for any affection he might give.

Now Matlakala lay in her bed, the covers tucked tightly under her armpits, her hands folded on her breasts, once again waiting. It was 3 am, and she couldn't sleep. A new day had begun, but she hadn't had the opportunity to put the previous day to rest. From her bed she could see her writing desk. A shaft of light from the streetlamp revealed her notepad, pens and computer. Her second novel was in there, lodged in the hard drive.

"Where was he?" she wondered. He usually came back around midnight. Matlakala clenched her hands as thoughts of what he could be doing played across her mind. She shut her eyes and breathed deeply – it was better not to know. When she opened them again they fell on her bridesmaid's dress hanging from the wardrobe door, still in its plastic cover. It was a lovely dress: pale purple chiffon and cut in an elegant style. Matlakala knew she'd look beautiful the day after tomorrow, when Ama married her love Thabo. She'd be there smiling and wishing them well like a best friend should. Maybe she would mean it, too, but right now she didn't feel like wishing anyone a happy life. It wasn't bitterness, but sometimes it felt like good things only ever happened to other people.

Ama was no beauty, and yet that hadn't prevented her from getting a proposal. She, Matlakala, was light skinned and attractive in a way that made men turn her way with appreciative glances. She couldn't help feeling that Ama didn't deserve what was happening in her life.

"God forgive me, jealousy is turning me into a bad person," Matlakala said out loud. What was wrong with her? Joe was her mistake; she couldn't blame anyone for her choice.

Fresh out of varsity, they had been young and in love. He was starting out in his career and she was writing her first novel. By the time she was published and the book had been declared a success, life was sweet. They bought a two bed-roomed house, small but big enough for the two of them.

Then Joe got retrenched. Matlakala would never forget the day it happened. She had known something was wrong the moment he stepped through the door. And things had not been the same since. Yet despite the way he treated her, she still loved him.

Suddenly her body stiffened and her heart jumped in her chest. She could hear footsteps outside on the pavement, and the jingle of keys. He was back. After some time the bedroom door opened, and she listened as he took off his clothes in the dark. The bed sank under his weight. His hands went to her, as she had expected. His alcohol-saturated body leant close, releasing its potent rye stench.

This was the closest he would get to her, late at night and drunk. He didn't speak, but he was gentle, and in a way it was enough. She leant into him, forgetting her woes.

Across town, Ama was also struggling to find sleep. She couldn't get the image of Pamela's unconscious body out of her mind, and the questions it raised that she didn't want to face. This was the first time she'd seen Pamela like that. All the other times Mandla had taken her to hospital himself. Why hadn't he taken her this time she wondered. Ama was a nurse and had seen worse, but seeing Pamela like that had scared her. If it hadn't been for Jeffrey, she wasn't sure how she'd have coped.

Giving up on sleep, she got up and reached for her gown from the chair next to her bed. In the sitting room, the quilt was there, almost complete, but waiting for the four women's hands to finish the last pieces. Ama sat down, picked up a red cloth and went back to work. It was sad, Ama thought. All this work for a wedding that was clouded by anger, pain, doubt and a love that she wished she could feel.

"Couldn't you sleep?" Jeffrey asked, coming to sit opposite his sister. "I was awake anyway, so I thought I should get on with this."

"You don't have to lie to me, sis," Jeffrey said. "Anyway, the quilt is pretty. I'm sure Thabo will appreciate it." He got to his feet. "Jeffrey?"
"Yes?"

"Do you think I'm doing the right thing, marrying Thabo? I mean would papa and mama approve?"

"It's a little too late to be thinking about that, sis. You're already traditionally married to him; the wedding is just a formality." Jeffrey's voice was tired. "You do love him, don't you?"

"I do," Ama said with conviction.

"Then there you have it," he said, leaving Ama working on the quilt that would be her wedding gift.

The sun slowly streaked the sky with shades of orange, purple, shimmering red and yellow. Beauty and Matlakala hurried down the street to Ama's house. It was early. They knew they still had a lot of work to do on the quilt. Beauty and Matlakala hardly spoke as they walked, each lost in thought. Ama watched them through the kitchen window and prepared herself, opening the door with a smile.

"Make us some coffee, will you? We need to get things started," Beauty said as she entered.

"By the way, is your brother in his room?"

"Yes," Ama said, frowning as she turned away to make the coffee. Beauty noticed her expression but ignored it, walking into Jeffrey's room. He was sprawled on the bed asleep. Beauty's heart skipped a beat. There was something about Jeffrey Bala that disarmed her. Even when he was asleep he seemed to still have power over her. Beauty walked to the bed and got under the covers to get close to him.

"Hi, beautiful," he said sleepily. "I waited for you last night, you didn't come."

"I had to go," she said.

"Did you miss me?" He turned to look at her, his eyes still half closed. Beauty felt herself tense at his words. It was always like this, as soon as he got too close.

"I think I should let you sleep. I'll be in the lounge with the girls." She placed a kiss on his forehead.

"I'll see you later then." He sighed before turning to go back to sleep. Beauty hesitated a moment before leaving.

In the sitting room, she could smell the freshly made coffee. She felt herself coming back to her usual self.

"Where is Pamela?" she asked, taking her place. Matlakala turned to Ama. She had been filled in about the early hours of the morning.

"She's in hospital," Ama said quietly, in a way that made Beauty feel she could not argue, or bring up the past or the deluge of insults that were fitting for that husband of Pamela's. They went on working in silence.

"Is she okay? I mean did he do a lot of damage?" Matlakala asked after a while.

"I couldn't tell. She seemed to be alright to me … I don't know," Ama said.

"Would you like some red underwear to go with that dress you've just picked, Ama? What does it matter?" Beauty asked. The other women turned to her, disbelief written on their faces. But before they could respond, they were intercepted by the noise coming from the construction of the tent in which the wedding reception was going to take place. "If you have nothing better to say please shut up." Beauty continued, disregarding the noise.

"You say the most hurtful things sometimes," Matlakala said.

"Really, Matlakala, I thought you would be used to people saying hurtful things to you by now? Oh, but I forgot. Joe doesn't really speak to you, does he?"

"Beauty, stop it," Ama said.

"I will, but know this: there's no point in discussing the degree of the beating because no matter what, it happened. Whether that bastard of a man broke her nose, her finger, even the smallest bone in her body, he had no right. So you discussing it doesn't make it better," she said, her anger suddenly subsiding. She looked at Matlakala, pitying her while at the same time feeling frustrated. But she said nothing.

From then on, they worked in silence, pressing on to finish the quilt in time. Tomorrow was the big day. Ama watched as cloth after cloth formed the patterns of her future. It was beautiful, and she felt strangely happy inside. The fears she'd felt a few hours ago were gone, she carried on working, content, soothed by the presence of her friends and the occasional clink of tools from outside. At about four o'clock in the afternoon they had finished. Their fingers were pierced by needles, but their faces beamed brightly at their hard work. Beauty even managed a few sentimental words. They spread out the quilt, tracing its unique patterns. While they were marvelling at the colours there was a knock at the door. Ama jumped up to open it. And there he was, the man who had been on her mind all day.

"Hi you," she said, smiling at him, suddenly forgetting her doubts.

"I need to talk you," Thabo said.

"Who is that?" Beauty walked to the door, coming between the couple. "Don't you know its bad luck to see the bride before the wedding day?" She pushed the door closed.

"Beauty, wait. I need to speak to her, it's important," Thabo said.

"It can wait." She closed the door.

"Hey!" Ama protested, trying to open the door, but Beauty stood with her back to it, blocking the way.

"You will thank me after the honeymoon. Create suspense, girl. Believe me, it works." She laughed. Ama smiled, but could not get the look on Thabo's face out of her mind. Something was clearly bothering him. She couldn't help feeling annoyed with Beauty. But he hadn't tried knocking again, so whatever it was couldn't have been that important.

Beauty felt her skin tingle where Jeffrey's hand brushed her back as they walked out the gate onto Maseru Street. Taxis crowded the street, carrying people returning from work. Red dust rose, mingling with the waning rays of the sun as the taxis came to a halt at the T-junction in front of the White Church. The disappointment and wariness she'd seen in Jeffrey's eyes that morning was gone. Now he seemed to be leading onto something else. Beauty didn't want to put a name to it, because it scared her. He was pushing her, she could feel it.

Their relationship, hardly a year old, was a ramshackle structure of loose dates, chance meetings, and passionate kisses that made them keep coming back for more, despite the lack of intimacy between them. The latter was a thorn in Beauty's side. Jeffrey had tried to move their relationship forward, but every time his kisses became more demanding, his touch more insistent, rough yet gentle at the same time, she'd retreat, offering some feeble excuse. It was fear so palpable her body wore its mark.

Beauty looked at Jeffrey as he walked next to her on their way to Dorothy Nyembe Park. They passed an old bus terminal on their right. The place was always packed with a long line of people trying their luck buying Lotto tickets or sitting on the steel benches, wiling away the day.

Jeffrey's hand moved to her back as he guided her across the road, and lingered as they walked on, passing an abandoned petrol station.

The sun was making its final descent from the sky as they approached the park, and Beauty felt giddy and soft inside, her other self forgotten. Here she was, a woman, feminine and sensual, yet all these feelings she kept to herself. She was afraid to let them out, afraid to let Jeffrey see; she feared giving him that power over her.

When he'd found her and the others still admiring the quilt, she'd wanted to jump into his arms and hold on to him forever. But she hadn't. Even now, walking with him to their favourite park was a joy she couldn't describe, but something as usual held her back.

"Did you hear what I said?" Jeffrey said.

"What?" she asked, embarrassed that she had not been listening, rather absorbing every sensation he wrought in her body and heart, because the fear of revealing herself to him wasn't the only one she felt. In the back of mind she knew their relationship would not last long, as there was no black man alive who'd go on like this. It was a miracle they had lasted this long.

"I said has Ama mentioned any trouble between her and Thabo?" Jeffrey repeated, his hand moving from her back to her shoulder, gently pulling her closer.

"No," Beauty said. "Well, not to me, anyway. Why do you ask?"

"No reason. I guess it's just brotherly concern."

"If there was trouble, he could have said so today," she said, remembering Thabo's quick visit.

"I guess," he said, guiding her through the open gate of the park. "Our bench is taken. Where shall we sit?"

Beauty eyed the couple carelessly sitting on their bench, with its view of the river. It was relaxing to watch the water's movements.

"There." Jeffrey pointed to the other side of the park. This side was dark. The lampposts automatically came on, making circles of light on the pavement. Finding an empty bench, they settled down. The mist wafted around them, fogging the spaces where the light didn't reach.

"This will do," he said, pulling her close. Beauty was silent, absorbing his comforting warmth.

"Hey, don't fall asleep."

"I won't." A giggle unexpectedly bubbled from her throat.

"Glad you think I'm funny." Jeffrey smiled.

"I'm not laughing at you. But I was actually thinking of taking a nap. I'm so tired."

"It's the quilt making that's making you tired," Jeffrey said, his hand making its way gently to Beauty's cheek. He looked her in the eyes, and once again Beauty felt like escaping. But she forced herself to keep still. Something was definitely on Jeffrey's mind.

"What are you thinking about?" she asked.

"Do you really want to know?" His hand paused on her chin.

"No," she said, apprehension squeezing her insides.

"I didn't think so." Jeffrey gave her a quick kiss on the lips, and settled comfortably on the bench. Beauty felt herself begin to relax again.

"How are the renovations going?" A few months ago Jeffrey had decided to open his own construction company. He had bought an old building in the CBD of Johannesburg.

Jeffrey looked at her for a long while, then seemed to give in to the change of subject.

"Not as fast as I would like. It seems I'll have to work from home for a few weeks."

"That's not so bad."

"Believe me, it is. I can't work with all the distractions around me."

"All you have to do is sit and draw."

"So you think being an architect is easy?" he said with a smile.

"Yes."

"Compared to what?" Now he was openly laughing.

"Have you ever had the misfortune of having to cope with hair gone bad? I deal with that every day."

"So you think I can't wield a comb?" He tugged her closer to him.

"What woman would trust you?" she asked, laughing.

"You."

The laughter died in her throat.

"One day you will trust me, Beauty. Now come, we have a big day tomorrow. My sister is getting married. Since I'm going to be giving her away, I need my rest."

"Yes," she said, getting to her feet. Trust. She didn't know if she was capable of that. She let Jeffrey guide her out of the park, feeling unsettled. He was becoming a threat to her peace of mind.

Chapter 3

Ama stood staring at herself in the mirror in amazement. This was her day, her wedding day. The white satin of her dress shimmered and slithered on her skin. A sheer veil covered her hair, which Beauty had curled into soft waves, creating an angelic look.

"You look beautiful, Ama," Matlakala said. Beauty stood apart from the others, appraising her handiwork. She'd woken up at dawn to create this vision in front of her. "I think it's time we got going," she said.

"Shouldn't we wait for Pamela?" Matlakala asked. The others ignored the question, pretending not to have heard her. As Ama readied to leave for the church, Beauty fussed around, fluffing the tail of the dress. Very soon she would be Mrs Thabo Maboa, she thought, with a shiver of excitement.

The three ladies made their way into the sitting room. The quilt they had finished yesterday lay there in its beauteous colours. Ama would give it to Thabo later that day, presenting it as a symbol of the submission of her body and soul to him. Tonight they would lie on it and get to know each other as husband and wife. Just a quilt, but it meant a lot to the four women, Ama thought. When they had started the tradition with Pamela, it had seemed like something fun, but it was then that they had begun to weave their friendship and love lives with colourful threads, which each craved would bring luck and love to the other. A gift of love it was.

Today Ama felt the gap created by Pamela's absence. She wanted her to be there, though she knew it wouldn't be appropriate for one of her bridesmaids to be covered in bruises so severe that she looked as though she'd been hit by a car.

"Are you ready, sis?" Jeffrey said, coming out of his room. He was wearing a charcoal suit and a white cotton shirt. "We should go now. It's getting …" He trailed off as the front door burst open. It was Pamela, her arm in a sling, her face coated with a thick layer of foundation in an attempt to conceal the red and black marks on her face. But the makeup only seemed to make the bruises stand out more. Matlakala rushed to her, but Pamela stopped her by raising her healthy hand. There was something wrong. From behind her, a man wearing a police uniform stepped into the doorway, squeezing past Pamela who seemed to be unable to move.

Ama sought her brother's shoulder.

"I think we should sit down," the officer said. He waited for them all to sit, looking down at his hands before clearing his throat. He seemed to be finding it difficult to say what he had come to say. He turned to Ama. "I presume you are Ama Bala," he said, nodding his own confirmation. "I regret to be the bearer of bad news, but your fiancé was found dead in the early hours of this morning. It looks like suicide, but we're still waiting on an autopsy to confirm. This is for you." The policeman reached into his breast pocket and pulled out a note. He passed it to Ama, who reached for it with a trembling hand.

"His family has already been notified, and they thought it best that I be the one to come and inform you. I'm sorry." He got to his feet. "I must be on my way. If you have any questions, the person to call is Detective Shai. I'll leave you his number. Thank you," he added unnecessarily, leaving the room.

Then there was silence as each tried to process the news.

Pamela was the first to say something. "Jeffrey, help your sister, please. Take her to her room. Matlakala, go and make her some tea. With lots of sugar."

Ama let her brother pull her up and guide her to her room. She felt like a robot. Time seemed to have stopped the moment the police officer stepped into the house.

She could feel her brother next to her, his breathing erratic. What was happening? Her mind pounded over and over again.

"Sit down," Ama heard Jeffrey say. She sat. The bed sank under her weight.

"Can I get you anything?" She heard him speak again, his deep voice cracking slightly. She wanted to respond, to ask what was happening, but the words seemed to be stuck. Her mind reeled with the policeman's words "found dead" and images of Thabo's face looking joyfully at her.

"Sis?" Jeffrey placed his hand gently on Ama's shoulder. "Shall I call Pamela? Do you want me to do that? Ama?" She still couldn't answer, and Jeffrey left the room.

Alone, the tears she'd been holding back fell, each one making its mark on her white satin dress. He was gone. Dead. She tried and failed to comprehend the word. How could it be? Whatever had been wrong, they could have worked it out. But wait! Her numbed mind echoed. She'd also had doubts, doubts strong enough to make her feel at times like she was suffocating. Doubt real enough to make her not want to marry him. But she'd swallowed them up, calling to mind their shared love and their good days. And she'd known she couldn't live without him. Had he not felt the same? Ama's hands flew to her burning eyes. Surely their love could have seen them through.

A thought then hit her. She was a widow. The lobola proceedings had been performed but a month ago. Ama had been so wrapped up in her own doubts and the wedding preparations that she had forgotten that, officially, she was already married. And now she was widowed! What did it all mean?

At that moment Pamela walked through the door.

Using her good arm to draw her near, she sat next to Ama, holding her head against her shoulder.

"I think I want to sleep," Ama said after a while.

Pamela nodded. "Let me help you with your dress."

Ama obliged, raising her arms so that Pamela could reach the zipper on the side of the dress. Ama helped Pamela gather the folds of her skirt up and over her head and then lay down in her undergarments, leaving

Pamela to deal with the dress. She closed her eyes, listening as Pamela move around the room.

"You know I'm a widow," she said.

"Traditionally I was married to him. We were married for thirty-two days, and I didn't even feel like his wife. Not yet, anyway. I was caught up with worries about the wedding, and my doubts. I kept waiting for this feeling to wash over me, and then I'd know he was my husband. But all that was for nothing, I was already his wife. And now I am a widow."

"Even so, Ama, your life will go on. You have to believe that for yourself."

"I wonder …" Ama opened her eyes and sat up. "I wonder what kind of life that will be, Pamela." She thought for a while, and then sighed. "But what choice do I have?"

"What do you mean, Ama?" Pamela said, sitting next to her on the bed.

"You live your life with broken bones and heavy make-up to cover up your bruises, yet you are living your life. There is still life for you after all that, isn't there?"

"This is not about me, Ama," Pamela said, touching her slung arm. It wasn't broken. This time it wasn't so bad.

"I know it's not about you. I have to be a widow, that's all. It can't be that complicated. I have to live alone without the burden or blessing of a husband. I don't have a choice in the matter. It's lonely nights I have to contend with. And you …"

"Yes me. I have fists for gratitude every day. But that's my life. Try to sleep, Ama. I will be in the sitting room if you need me."

"Aren't you going to be late? Mandla might …"

"He can wait. Besides, he won't do anything – his punching bag is not healthy yet. Don't worry about me, Ama, just get some rest," she said, walking out of the room.

Ama lay back. She was exhausted, but her mind was too full to sleep, and she laid there, images of Thabo's face swimming before her closed eyes.

In the sitting room, Matlakala turned to Pamela as she entered. "How is she?" she asked, her voice low.

"She'll be fine. Where is Jeffrey?" Pamela asked.

"He went to inform the guests."

"That's good."

"What happens now, Pamela?"

"Don't be stupid, Matlakala. What kind of question is that?" Beauty snapped.

"Beauty, please, don't start. We have to stick together for Ama, okay?"

The door opened and Jeffrey came in. His handsome face was pained as he looked at the three women "Thabo's uncle is outside and he's asked everyone to go to the church. They are having a gathering there. So if you ladies could get your things, we can go."

"What about Ama?" Pamela asked. "Surely they don't expect her to go?"

"I think she can be excused for now," he said. "But we better get going. Everybody is already making their way to the church."

The short drive to the church was tolerated silently. Everybody in the car felt misplaced, and out of sorts. Here they were, dressed colourfully, as if for a wedding, and yet now it was more like a funeral. The inside of the church accentuated the irony. It was a beautiful church decorated for a beautiful wedding, but everywhere one turned tearful faces stared back as a reminder of what had happened. Jeffrey and the three friends found seats near the front. Thabo's family was there. His mother, colourfully clad in her traditional garb, fought with her tears, while his father talked softly to his brother-in-law at his side, both their heads bowed. On his other side was Thabo's older brother. None of the women had met him before, and there were rumours that there was something not quite right about him.

"Firstly, I would like to thank you for coming," someone was saying. It was Thabo's father, now standing behind the pulpit. "It is with great sadness in my heart that I am standing here saying words that will send my son into deep rest rather than into a beautiful marriage." He wiped a tear that trickled down his cheek. "As soon as his body is released by the police, Thabo will be buried. Your support as shown today will be greatly appreciated. The pastor would like to say a few words. Thank you." His voice wavered a little on the last words. The pastor took his place at the pulpit. He read a few words of comfort from the Bible and said a prayer.

The congregation dispersed and the four moved forward to offer their condolences to Thabo's family.

Pamela spoke in soft soothing tones, lingering longer with Thabo's mother. Jeffrey held Thabo's father's hand and felt the clasp tighten

"It is my worst day as a father," he repeated. A man came forward and placed his hand on Thabo's father's shoulder.

"I'm Thabo's uncle." He addressed Jeffrey. "You might have seen me during the lobola proceedings." Jeffrey nodded.

"The family is going to have a meeting about what should be done about Ama," he said.

"Brother, this is not the time. Can't we leave everything for tomorrow? The girl is still in shock. We still have funeral arrangements to make. The sooner the better, I think."

Thabo's father rubbed at his eyes. He patted Jeffrey before helping his wife to her feet and making for the church doors, his older son close behind them.

"Let's go." Jeffrey turned to the ladies waiting for him, seeking Beauty's hand.

Back at Ama's house, Pamela and Matlakala hurried into her room to check on Ama.

"Maybe I should see if she's okay too." Beauty said, but Jeffrey pulled her back. "No." He held on tight. "She has all the friends she needs." He led Beauty to his bedroom. "Please, I need a friend too," he said, opening the door.

"Jeffrey?" Beauty said nervously.

"Come." He took off his jacket, closing the door behind him

"Jeffrey, I don't …"

"Shhh, just let me hold you. For a little while, help me forget what's happened to my sister." He pulled her closer. Gently, they lay down on the bed holding each other. Beauty's body tensed up, afraid to move.

"Relax," he said gently. "I'm not going to do anything to you."

"I know," she lied, her heart racing.

Ama stared up at the ceiling. This couldn't be real. Surely someone would come and wake her soon, to tell her it had all been a bad dream. She sat up and reached for the letter Thabo had left for her. It felt heavy in her hands. He was gone. Forever. Lying back down, she felt like crying. But the tears wouldn't come, and she went back to staring at the ceiling.

Chapter 4

Ama woke up with a massive headache pounding at her temples. Her were eyes puffy, her throat dry. She sat at the edge of the bed with a vague memory of Pamela and Matlakala being in her room. Absentmindedly she reached for her gown, and threaded her arms through the sleeves. On the bedside lay Thabo's letter, untouched.

The house was strangely quiet. No radio played, and not even the television was switched on. Was every soul in mourning? Ama asked out loud.

It almost sounded like a joke to her. How was it that she couldn't feel the pain of her loss? Maybe she was still in shock, she thought, walking through the sitting room where Jeffrey was sprawled on the couch, asleep. Ama's heart strings pulled; he must have been exhausted.

Ever since the wedding preparations had started he hadn't slept properly. He had taken on all the roles that other relatives would normally fill, if they had had any.

Jeffrey had been the negotiating uncle, the stern, proud father, and reassuring mother. And for what, Ama asked herself, stopping to look at his sleeping form.

Ama seized her thoughts and began making coffee. Setting out two oversized mugs, she poured in the coffee and carried them both to the sitting room. There she nudged Jeffrey with her toe. He woke up, opening one eye, and then reached for the coffee, mumbling his thanks.

"You could have slept in your room," Ama said sitting next to him.

"Ah, well, I sort of landed here after Beauty and the others left." He righted himself on the sofa.

"You okay?" he asked after a while.

"I don't know," she said honestly.

"It will get better."

"I know."

They had been here before, when their parents died. Devastating as it had been, they had survived. But this was different: Ama was in it alone. Jeffrey wished he knew what to say to her.

"The Maboa family is going to have a meeting tomorrow about what's to be done for you."

"Oh?"

"Yeah," he said, sipping his coffee.

"It's not necessary. He's dead. There's nothing they can do about that," Ama said.

"We'll see." Jeffrey sighed. "You know what goes into these things."

"No, I don't know, Jeffrey. Do you?"

"I'm not sure, Ama, but I don't think there's anything to worry about. Try to relax," he said, patting her on her back.

Strangely, sitting there with her brother, Ama felt almost content. With him, she had no role to play. She was not a widow, or an almost wife. She was simply who she had always been.

"It's going to take some time to clean up everything," Jeffrey said.

"Tomorrow I'll call up Pamela and the others. We'll have the yard clean in no time. I'll have to figure out where to take the food."

"The funeral is going to be soon. Thabo's father said so."

"Well … the better for it."

"Yeah?"

"There's no need to prolong things. It's done, isn't it?"

"Not entirely."

"What's left, Jeffrey?"

"You."

"What do you want me to do?"

"Nothing … I just want to see you okay, that's all" Jeffrey rubbed his temples. "The thing is, I can only guess at what you're feeling. I …"

"It's alright, Jeffrey. I'll be fine. Right now I'm feeling a bit numb, but I'll be okay."

"You sure?"

"Jeffrey. Can we not talk about this for a while?"

"Okay, I'll be quiet."

"That's all I need," Ama said, snuggling into his shoulder.

Pamela sat in front of her dressing table. The mirror reflected a face she hardly knew. Her eyes scanned the layers of make-up carefully applied to conceal the bruises beneath. The powder formed grotesque patterns on her stitched cheek. She would be lucky if it didn't get infected.

Who is that in the mirror, she wanted to ask herself. She had no answer. It was her, of course. She had to believe it was her. Or she'd know how much she'd lost. At this thought, Ama's face and the morning's events came to mind. She'd woken in the early hours of dawn, her mind focused on seeing her friend off into marriage. Her movements slowed by her injuries, she'd sat at this chair and done what she could to cover up the marks on her face. She hadn't been able to hide them completely, but she looked better – at least that's what her eyes told her at the time. She'd stood up and decided to go to Thabo's house to make up for wasted time. Mandla had been awake then. He'd witnessed her departure with little interest.

At Thabo's house she arrived just in time to catch the wedding party leaving for the church. And then the police officer had arrived. The family had disappeared into the house.

It was Thabo's uncle who went out to inform the waiting friends and family. He had been as tactful as one could be in such a situation. But before he began speaking he couldn't help but undo his colourful tie, removing the last remnants of the joyous day. And then he'd said it – Thabo was dead.

Pamela hadn't wanted Ama to hear the news from the police officer. She had rushed, taking a taxi to beat the police officer to Ama's house. She had almost succeeded, only to see him there in his uniform seconds after she had arrived. It hadn't helped, Pamela thought, sitting there staring at herself in the mirror. Her tears had made black streaks of mascara on her cheeks. She wiped at them with a tissue, removing some of her make-up in the process to reveal the black and blue marks below. Pamela clenched her jaw, and consciously straightened her spine, adjusting her defeated stance. She needed to stay strong.

As she began reapplying her make-up, she heard Mandla's calculated steps coming towards the bedroom. She was so tuned into him, she could sense when he was approaching the other side of the house. It would have been romantic if it wasn't for the fear pricking her insides, making her heart race and her stomach churn.

Her husband had during the course of their marriage become a tyrant. They had been two years into their marriage, their son Sizwe two years old, when Mandla had changed. Thirteen years had come and gone. When her sons had been young, they had been a buffer and a shield from her husband's abuse. But now Sizwe was grown up and was leading his own life. And her other sons, Sihle and Njabulo, were preoccupied with schoolwork and friends.

Pamela picked up her face powder to keep busy as Mandla turned the knob to open the door. He sauntered in, like a king entering his palace, his handsome face hard and unyielding. That face was what had first attracted her to him, Pamela thought, trying her hardest to ignore him.

"You clean up good, don't you?" he said sitting down at the edge of the bed, and watching her in the mirror. Pamela stared back at him, wondering whether he expected an answer to his mocking question. Mandla held her gaze for some time, challenging, and then he laughed, throwing himself back on the bed, his fingers intertwined behind his head.

"I heard about your friend," he said. "If you hadn't been in such a rush to leave this morning I could have told you were wasting your time when there wasn't going to be a wedding."

"What do you mean, Mandla? How did you know that?" Pamela suddenly felt cold.

"Really, Pamela, are you so stupid? Those two were never going to work. I'm surprised you couldn't see that. I've never seen a man so unhappy. I'm not surprised he did what he did." Pamela looked at him, incredulous. How could anyone be so callous?

She got to her feet and walked to her wardrobe. Feeling shaky, she pulled at her dress. She struggled to think of something to say, knowing that her silence would only annoy him more, but her mind was blank. She removed her dress, careful of her hurt arm, revealing large black and blue bruises covering her back and across her chest. She heard Mandla muttering in disgust behind her, and quickly pulled on a shirt, wincing at the fast movement. Her arm back in its sling, Pamela turned to face her husband. She could see he was angry, waiting for anything that could start a fight. She turned to the door, making her movements as casual as possible, trying not to let her nerves show.

"You should tell your friend to mind her own business." Pamela's back tensed as she turned to face him.

"What do you mean by that?" she asked cautiously.

"I mean I don't like sneaky women meddling in my business. If I'd thought you needed to go to hospital, I would have taken you." Mandla got off the bed and advanced menacingly. "Was it you who called her?"

Pamela blinked. Sizwe, her son, had called Ama. Mandla didn't know that.

"Yes," she said in a whisper, thinking of her son. Mandla was close now. "I didn't think you'd care who took me," she continued in a low tone, trying to keep calm.

"I won't have you taint my reputation, do you hear?" Pamela nodded, her eyes filling with tears. She turned to open the door, almost colliding with Sizwe as she passed his room. Previously an RDP house, over the years various rooms had been added. Now it was like a maze, with sudden turning corners and random pillars placed to support the roof where walls had been demolished. Nevertheless, Pamela had made it homey, painting the walls in a peach colour and adding tasteful decorations.

"Hey!" she said, putting on a cheerful face. Her son stared at her questioningly.

"I'm going to start supper, what would you like today?"

"I'm not hungry," he said, looking down at the bat he was holding. Her son was in love with cricket.

"Even so, you should eat. You know food never goes to waste in this house." Pamela looked around in the kitchen.

"I thought you'd died last night."

Pamela froze in her tracks. She didn't know what to say to him. She couldn't promise that it wouldn't happen again. Sizwe was beyond such lies.

"Don't think about that. Forget it happened." His shoulders slumped. Pamela's heart ached at his expression.

"Do you know what he did after beating you? He watched TV for two hours. Then he drove off somewhere. And I had to watch you lying on that floor, praying that you'd wake up. You were so still, I thought you must be dead. Then I thought, wouldn't it be better if she were dead? I felt free then, when you didn't wake up. But I have two brothers, and they still need you." He paused, looking up at Pamela, his eyes narrowing. "The only sad thing is that you don't need them enough to stay alive, mom." He began to walk away from her, swinging the bat at his side.

"Sizwe"

"Don't explain yourself to me. You don't have to."

And he was gone. Pamela stared forlornly after him, not knowing what to say or do. There being no answer, she started on her cooking.

Matlakala took a few deep breaths to steady her emotions.

Her hands trembled, closing the pages of the magazine she had been reading. The weathered pages showed their frequent handling. She was sitting in Beauty's hair salon, waiting for her to close up.

Despite the day's events, Beauty had opened shop. "Death is a traveller," she'd said. "One minute he's here, the next he's gone. Why should we wait for him to return?" Beauty had been callous about the whole thing, Matlakala thought, as she was with many things. Nothing seemed to touch her. She was a granite rock defying the scarring effects of time: never fall, never falter.

Matlakala observed her putting extensions in a client's hair. Her hands moved fast, switching and twirling the braids into place. Beauty was talented, Matlakala acknowledged. It was just that she could be so hard. Matlakala watched as she chatted away to the client, the day's events forgotten.

When they had left Ama's house, grief stricken, Matlakala had decided to go along with Beauty, not wanting to face the hours alone. She'd known Joe wouldn't be there to help her forget. Matlakala had hoped, when she'd tagged along with Beauty, that they'd talk, cry a little, and comfort each other, as women often did. But there had been none of that. Tears welled up in Matlakala's eyes. Her fingers worried the folds of her purple bridesmaid's dress; she felt out of place in the spotless and sophisticated salon. All around her, life went on, when it felt like hers was being turned upside down. Nothing was as it should be. At least she still had Joe, she thought. Yet she felt very much alone. Fighting back tears, she gathered her things, and slowly made her way to the door. Her head hurt from all the tears she refused to let fall. She couldn't cry here, not where Beauty would see her being weak. She left without saying goodbye.

Beauty watched her leave and felt her throat tighten. She stilled herself, busying her hands with the braids. Her heart felt heavy in her chest and she could feel her anxiety levels rising, making it harder than usual to hide her nerves. Beauty felt like she was cracking up. Multiple thoughts raced through her mind, chief among them Jeffrey. She could not allow herself to fall under his spell, especially now, when it was so tempting to seek some warmth and comfort. She had to hold on to her fears, use them as a shield. Thabo was dead, Jeffrey was alive, she was alive, but she couldn't let him in. An emotion she couldn't name bubbled in the pit of her stomach rushed up; she released a pained sigh to ease it away. Her eyes roamed around the salon, landing where Matlakala had sat. Beauty hadn't meant to ignore her. It was just that she couldn't allow herself to cry. She felt that if she did, she wouldn't stop.

Outside it was growing dark. Beauty twisted the extensions into a stylish hairdo. Thirty minutes later she was done, her client gone and she stepped into the house for the first time that morning. Her mother must have been in the kitchen, because there were dinner pots on the stove. But she couldn't think of food: all she wanted was the haven of her room.

"Beauty?" Her mother was standing in the doorway. As usual, she let her come to her. Beauty picked around her room in the dark.

"How is Ama?" she asked.

Beauty sighed. "She'll survive, I guess. It goes to show: nothing is ever concrete in this world. Even people who are meant to be together are not together. What is going to happen to us? It is the worst for black women: we hope for something that doesn't exist in our race. If it's not polygamy, it's alcoholism," Beauty said, her tone bitter.

"Now if that's your view, tell me exactly what is it you're doing with that boy, Jeffrey?" The question caught Beauty off guard.

"I don't know."

"You would want him to love you one day, though?" Mma Maluse insisted.

"Is love something I'll ever want?"

"Of course." Beauty's mother took her hand and pulled her to the bed. "It starts with you, baby. The comfort he gives you, you can only give back."

"It's not that simple, Ma." she said, thinking of how she'd felt earlier in Jeffrey's arms.

"Yes, it is."

"But I get so scared. I feel overwhelmed and out of control."

"Are you afraid of what he might do?"

"No, it's … I can't explain it. I just get scared"

"It'll get better."

That's if he doesn't leave me first, Beauty thought.

"Open your heart to him, it will get better," Mma Maluse said, as though she'd heard her thoughts. After all that had happened to her, Beauty's mother was still positive about life, about people. But still Beauty couldn't open her heart to anyone. It was too risky.

That night Beauty lay awake for hours, before finally falling asleep, holding her fears close.

Chapter 5

The sun unfolded its water-coloured canvas to the horizon, bringing forth another day. Matlakala turned to lie on her back in the bed, rolling over onto Joe's side. The sheets were cold, chilling her body. He hadn't come home last night. Matlakala's eyes ached from a long night of crying. She was tempted to stay in bed all day, but the need to pee and the thought of a long, hot bath got her up. On the way to the bathroom, she was stopped in her tracks. Her mouth opened in surprise. Joe was sprawled on the bathroom floor, passed out. Vomit trailed from the toilet to the floor near his head. She felt both pity and disgust. He was like a little boy now, helpless, reduced to idiocy by a mere bottle of fermented barley.

"Joe!" A pained cry escaped from her throat, and she fell to her knees beside him. Her hands moved over her boyfriend's still form, trying to lift him up. The pressure of her pulling roused him from his drunken stupor. One blood-shot eye opened, then another, meeting Matlakala's tender stare. For a moment, he stared at her, shame faced. Matlakala could tell that he was vulnerable: His face was a collage of the shame and the hatred he felt for himself. He closed his eyes, and when he opened them they were filled with anger. He pushed himself up, wiping at his face and muttering something under his breath as he pushed past Matlakala. She stepped aside, an apology escaping her lips.

"Sorry," she repeated to the empty space. But he was gone.

The yard was a mess, Ama thought, her hands on her hips. Her eyes scanned the clustered space: she hadn't thought that cleaning up would be such hard work. The preparations for the wedding hadn't been this tedious. Pamela wasn't much help with her injured arm, either. She left all the heavy lifting to Ama, and with all the lifting she was getting tired quickly, without much progress apparent. Ama sat down on one of the plastic chairs, which the wedding planner was coming later to collect.

This was all so wrong, Ama thought. All the guests who had come to see her married were nowhere in sight. If there had been a wedding, today she'd be on her honeymoon, enjoying the fruits of marriage. They had planned to go to the Kruger National Park, a week of nothing but wild life.

Now, instead of a relaxing holiday, she would be planning a funeral.

But right now, she couldn't allow herself to mourn him. Not yet, a voice inside kept saying.

"Do you think we'll ever finish?" Pamela's voice came to Ama from far away. She was bent over a pot, scooping out steaming beef stew into an oversized container. She sounded worn out.

"If we can get rid of the food today, I'll be happy. The rest we'll see to tomorrow."

"I won't be here tomorrow, Ama. I'm sorry, but I can't miss another day of work."

"Looking like that? What will your boss say?"

Pamela could imagine the look of distaste, the expression that seemed to imply she had brought this on herself. He would mutter something about "upholding images" and would probably confine her to the office for a few weeks, away from the curious, complacent tourists that poured out to view the twisted streets and memorable sites of Soweto. But the alternative to this humiliation was dealing with Mandla, who would accuse her of being a lazy gold-digger if she took too much time off work.

Ama caught Pamela's train of thought. "Don't think too much about it, Pam. Maybe he'll understand."

"I doubt it." Pamela's voice caught, giving in to the emotions she rarely showed. "I tell myself all the time: 'Your strength is in you, you hold the key to your life no matter what he does. Your life is your children; as long as they are fine you'll be fine.' It used to be enough. I had my job, my kids, and my life. I couldn't ask God for more. No black woman could. Mandla has made my life insignificant, alienated me from my children, my work, and shamed me as a woman. I ..." she sniffed, and her eyes lowered.

"I'm sorry. Here I am going on about myself when you ... It's just that Thabo's death has knocked me upside down."

"Please let's not speak about him, at least not yet."

"I understand." Pamela smiled weakly. "So what are we going to do about the food?"

Ama placed her hands on Pamela's rounded cheeks, gently grazing the stitched area. "Why don't you leave him while you still have both your feet to do so?"

"I've tried that before, remember." Pamela sighed "The last thing I want is a bullet rusting in my decomposing body and my children growing up without a mother because I was selfish, to seek my own happiness."

"But it's no way to raise kids, Pamela, the way things are. You know that. If Sizwe saw what I saw on Thursday night ..."

"Yes, I know Ama, but would you rather they grew up without a mother? Brainwashed into thinking I didn't love them? The only way I could leave that man is in a coffin."

"Mandla wouldn't do that, Pam." Words were easy to say, Ama thought, remembering the image of Pamela's bloodied body lying unconscious on the floor. In the back of her mind, she wondered what Thabo had looked like when the police had found him, wherever they'd found him. She realised that the police officer who had come to inform them of his death had not said where they'd found him. Maybe she should have asked.

"What are you ladies doing?" Both women turned around to find Beauty standing there. They brushed at their faces, trying to erase any sad emotions.

Beauty had seen their bent heads from afar, and her heart had pulled at the sight. Thabo's death had been a blow to all of them. Even her mother seemed bothered, with her questions and insistent pushing in a direction Beauty didn't want to go. The latter thought brought Jeffrey to mind. Beauty wondered where he was. The last time she saw him he hadn't been well. His sister's situation had hit him hard. Beauty longed to see him, see if he was okay.

"We are tired. We thought you'd be here earlier to help out."

"I had to deal with my mother, she was having one of her excited days," Beauty said. Ama and Pamela nodded. None of Beauty's friends had met her, and she rarely spoke about her to anyone, becoming defensive when people asked about her.

"Where is Matlakala? I thought you were going to come with her," Pamela said.

"She said something about a deadline tomorrow. I thought she'd call you."

"I thought she wasn't even halfway with her book," Ama said.

Pamela shook her head. "What did Joe do this time?" She seemed to be speaking to herself. There was an awkward silence. Beauty bit her tongue, looking at Pamela's bruised face.

"What can I do to help?" Beauty changed the topic.

"The food: we don't know what to do with it," Ama said. If there was no way out the food will go to waste in a day.

"Well," Beauty said, her eyes scanning the full containers. "We could take it to Joburg, give it to some street kids."

"Where would we go? Joburg is big," Pamela asked.

"The Bridge, maybe. It's busy. We'll finish quickly."

"Ama, what do you think?" Pamela asked, her reluctance showing.

"Anything to get rid of it."

"Let's go then."

The three women got to work carrying the containers out to Ama's car. Before they left, Ama went back into the house to fetch her car keys and cellphone. She stopped for a while staring at her phone, thinking for a moment, as she had many times since his death, that Thabo might call. And then remembering. She breathed in deeply, and closed the door behind her.

Matlakala stared at the screen. She couldn't allow herself to think about Joe, because once she did, he would be there all day, hijacking her thoughts and making it impossible to write. She began writing, her fingers moving rapidly over the keyboard.

I once heard a man being beaten to death. I was standing in a long line of commuters when I heard his screams, echoing in the cavernous space of the Soweto taxi rank. I could almost feel his pain, and yet the people around me seemed unaware that anything had happened. A man was dead, and we were preoccupied with getting ourselves safely home.

Matlakala looked at her words on the screen. Despite the violence of the scene, and the thoughts it had brought to mind, clicking the save button, she felt strangely calm.

Chapter 6

Three days had passed, and still Ama was silent. Jeffrey was getting worried. But all he could do was watch her, and be ready for her when she allowed herself to let go. It was hard. They were living in the same house like strangers, each mindful of the other, but not sure what to say.

This was strange territory for him, Jeffrey thought while observing his sister silently preparing their dinner. When he'd told her about Thabo's upcoming funeral that Saturday, she had barely reacted. Her response had been a vague shake of her head. Jeffrey didn't know what to do. Not long ago, they had been in the same situation, when they'd buried their parents, but then she had reached out to him, letting him know how much pain she felt, and they had healed each other. Now everything was different: it was as though he wasn't there.

"You can stop staring now, Jeffrey, the food is ready." Ama smiled. It had been a while since he'd seen anything but sadness on her face.

"What?"

"The way you were staring at me, you'd swear I was about to poison your food."

"Oh no, I was just thinking."

"You haven't told me what Thabo's family has decided."

"Oh." Jeffrey was surprised at her bringing up anything to do with Thabo. "Well I don't know anything yet," he said, sitting down at the table.

Ama was quiet for a while, as she filled their plates.

"But you told me they were going to have a meeting on Sunday?"

"Yes, there was, but I wasn't invited."

"You've been there all week helping with the funeral preparations. Hasn't anyone said anything?"

Jeffrey looked up from his plate. He searched her eyes, and could see the fear in them. "Don't worry about it, sis. They'll say something when it's time. They'll probably want to have some sought of cleansing ceremony. You mustn't worry about it."

"You know I don't believe in those things, Jeffrey. I am a Christian. I don't believe in these traditional rituals. I never have and I'm not going to start now just because Thabo decided to kill himself."

"I know that, Ama. But they are his family. The main thing is just to get through this, so you can move on with your life. This thing has been hanging in the air for a while now. Thabo will be buried on Saturday and we can all move on."

"You really think it's that simple?"

Jeffrey sighed, reaching across the table for Ama's hand. "Of course not. We both know nothing is ever that simple. I'm just tired. The sooner this is over the better."

"I just don't like my life being in other people's hands, that's all."

"I can understand that. Look, hopefully they'll tell us tomorrow. You are going to the viewing, right?"

"Yes I am. His mother came this afternoon to ask me in person. So I have to be there."

There was a knock at the door.

"Were you expecting anyone?" she asked, not moving.

"Yes, I invited Beauty over."

"You didn't tell me."

Jeffrey looked at her questioningly, opening the door for Beauty. He could tell she was uncomfortable. He was never sure what to expect with her. "Come in," he said with a smile. She smiled back at him, transforming her face. If only she knew how beautiful she was, Jeffrey thought. She had dressed up a little, and was wearing some make-up and a wrap-around dress that showed off her small waist.

"We were just finishing dinner. There's still some more pap and vleis, if you want to join us." Jeffrey ushered Beauty to a chair, and Ama fetched another plate. They ate their food, chatting amicably. Beauty relaxed a bit, absorbing the easy warmth shared between sister and brother, although she could tell sense some tension in Ama.

After her coffee, Ama left the two still at the table and went to her room. Alone, her thoughts turned to Thabo. It was strange: she could feel the void he had left, as if she had never existed without him. And yet when he had been alive, she'd doubted her feelings for him. The love they had shared hadn't seemed to be enough for her. She had searched for something or someone who could produce an emotion in her she didn't know it was possible to feel. She had lacked faith. And now he was gone, and she wasn't sure if she had ever found that feeling.

Her hand went to the dressing table. She picked up the letter he had left for her. Throughout the week she had sat on her bed staring at it, lacking the courage to read its contents. It wasn't fair, she thought. Why hadn't he said something to her before he died? This wasn't enough: a cold piece of paper giving his reasons for being unable to live his life with her, if that was what this was.

Ama tossed the letter back on the dressing table, disgusted. She didn't want to hear any justifications for what he had done. She didn't want to be made to understand his actions. No! She wasn't going to let him take everything, even her anger. He could burn in hell for all she cared. She had planned a wedding for six months, and what did she have to show for it! A lonely bed and a funeral on Saturday. To hell with Thabo Maboa, Ama shouted in her mind.

And his mother could forget her tearful suggestion of remaining friends even though Ama hadn't married her son. She had come that afternoon unexpectedly, apologising for not visiting earlier. She was embarrassed and ashamed, she'd said. She had felt all the things a mother feels when her son had been caught committing the most brutal crime, against a woman at that, as if he didn't have a mother he cared about. It was a betrayal, worse than any she'd experienced in her life, she'd said.

In many ways, Thabo's mother's feelings matched hers. In those moments, the pain they felt as individuals brought them together as they sat, mourning the man they had known and loved. It wasn't uncommon for the daughter to comfort the mother. But, seeing the other woman's pain, for the first time Ama was unable to ignore her own, and at last she had cried for him. The older woman's arms around her, she began to let it out, allowing herself to remember Thabo and their life together. It was a release to feel some pain, but she could not forgive him. She was less sad than she was angry with him. And right now, her anger kept him alive.

And yet she felt guilty, too. Maybe she hadn't loved him as he deserved. All this time she had blamed him for the fact that things weren't perfect; she'd put all the responsibility of their relationship on him. Even in his death, she was doing the same thing, wanting him to take care of her even when it wasn't possible. His mother had said much the same thing. She had shown Ama a picture of her older son and told her that Thabo had been like a firstborn, taking care of everybody, including his older brother. Thabo's mother had mentioned Thabo's brother's name, but Ama couldn't remember it.

The older brother in the picture looked nothing like Thabo. He looked blank, as though the photographer had edited out his emotions. His features faded away while she was still looking at the picture. Ama didn't know why Thabo's mother had decided to show it to her. It seemed unfair that she should flaunt her blessings in front of Ama. Who did she have left? She thought of her brother with Beauty in the living room, and felt a wave of self pity wash over her. She got under the covers, hoping sleep would help to drain away some of her sorrow. Loneliness was hard to bear, especially as the days that came and went and everyone else moved on with their lives.

Beauty lay on the bed, absorbing every kiss, every word that Jeffrey offered. His hands were gentle on her skin, and she felt herself start to relax. Before she had accepted Jeffrey's invitation to spend the night together, Beauty had struggled with the idea of accepting or refusing his offer. The latter would have been the easy way out. And their relationship would be right where it had been for the past year, and her fears of losing him an increasing likelihood. What did they say about a woman refusing a man? Sex was considered to be the basis of most relationships, after all. But it was what Beauty feared most: the idea of letting a man touch her and discover the thing she'd hidden all her life. The thought was unimaginable.

And in some ways with Jeffrey it was worse, because of what she had to lose. What would he think when he saw her body, saw it all? She thought about the questions he might ask. She couldn't bear to talk about what had happened. Not to anyone, and especially not Jeffrey. He would see too deep, too far, where she didn't want anyone to see.

She thought of her mother, a woman who had probably forgotten what the touch of a lover felt like, and not by choice. With her mother, there was no hiding what she had been through. Mma Maluse's face, though healed, bore the ugly scars that would never go away, and she was still unable to use her right arm, despite intense physiotherapy. Yet she faced the world as though nothing was wrong with her. Beauty knew that her mother had not forgotten, and that she did not hold onto the past.

Lying in Jeffrey's arms, Beauty knew the only remedy was to face her fears. She felt his hands touching her where they had not touched before, but tonight it felt okay. His hands were reassuring and caring, and she breathed in deeply, allowing herself to be lulled by his tenderness, and gradually becoming less conscious of what he was doing, even as he began to lift up her dress.

His hand glided on her body, gently exploring, and then paused. He propped himself up on one elbow. "What's this?" Jeffrey asked.

Beauty cringed, then quickly covered herself with her dress and wiggled away from him, her body rigid. "Beauty!" She could see the worry in his face. "What is it?"

"I'm leaving," Beauty said. But she didn't move.

"Beauty?" Jeffrey said again, reaching for her hand, which she pulled away. She rolled over, staring at the wall, fighting back tears. This scar had stolen so much from her: her laughter, her childhood, her and her mother's chance at a normal life. Jeffrey's hand reached for her again, trying to pull her to face him.

"Don't," Beauty said. It would have been so easy to melt into his touch, and part of her craved it. But it wouldn't change the reality of her life: she was scarred from the inside out.

"Beauty, I just want you to talk to me. I want to understand you. I thought you wanted this." She could hear the hurt and confusion in his voice.

He waited for her to respond, but she couldn't speak. After a while, he sighed and got up. "I'll take you home."

Beauty watched him put on his clothes. When he was finished, she waited for him to say something. She wanted him to ask her again and again, even though she knew she would never answer him. Beauty bit her lip, trying to think of something to say, but no words came, and instead she stood up to follow Jeffrey.

The ride home was strained by unsaid words. Beauty shrank into her seat, grateful for the darkness of the car. She trained her eyes forward, not daring to look at Jeffrey. This will be over soon, she silently said to herself. She should have known better than to let her guard down.

They were almost there. The drone of the engine came to a halt, and she groped for her things, reaching for the door handle. Light flooded into the car as the door opened. She looked at Jeffrey. His face was expressionless.

"Goodnight," she said.

"I'll walk you," he said, coming round to her side and taking her hand firmly in his, giving her no choice but to follow. At the front door, she turned to face him. She was getting a little nervous. She could see a shadow moving at the front window. "Goodnight Jeffrey," she said again. But he remained where he was. Her hand shaking slightly, she unlocked the door.

"Aren't you going to switch on the lights?"

"Um, yes." For years she'd walked in and out of the house in darkness; she'd never had the need to switch them on. Feeling for the switch, she pressed it, and then there was light. Shadows disappeared and bad memories evaporated. Jeffrey pushed through the door to come in, and walked ahead to the kitchen. Beauty sensed a shift in his mood, from concern to frustration.

"Tell me," he said, leaning against the sink and folding his arms across his chest, "How is it that when I think we're moving forward, I find myself right back where we started?"

Beauty turned to him, dragging the door shut.

"I don't think I have to answer your question," she said, matching his stance.

"I know you don't have to, but I thought maybe you might want to. If you wanted things to work out with us. But maybe you don't."

Beauty was silent. Jeffrey looked at her for a long time, then shook his head.

"Goodnight, Beauty." He pushed away from the sink. Sadness invaded the space, old shadows regaining their form.

"Jeffrey," Beauty heard herself say.

"Yes?" His hand reached out, hovering just above hers. They were there, his fingers and palm, but not touching her.

"Beauty?" Her mother's voice filled the silence.

"Who's that?" he asked, pulling back his hand and turning towards the passageway. "I thought you lived here alone?" His gaze came back to her.

Beauty stared at him, feeling trapped. Like a cornered animal, she wanted to flee. This was too much, in one night. Before she could come up with something to say, the voice came again.

"Beauty?" She sounded agitated. Her mother was used to being answered when she called.

"Yes, Ma." Beauty's eyes stayed on Jeffrey's face. She could hear her mother shuffling down the darkened passageway.

"It's my mother. Now please will you leave?"

"Don't you want me to meet her?"

"Jeffrey, please, not now." She stepped in front of him, blocking his view of the passage. To her relief, he didn't push.

"Alright, Beauty, I'm going. But we need to talk about this."

"Thank you," she said softly. "Ma, I'm coming now," she called down the passage, walking Jeffrey to the door.

He left, not turning to look back at her.

Switching off the light, Beauty went to her mother. Old shadows settled in, resumed their long acquired residence as Beauty walked back down the passage in the dark.

Chapter 7

The sad day anticipated by many had arrived, matched by the cold Soweto skies, which poured down on the hunched mourners.

Ama rebelled at the feelings that threatened to engulf her. She had promised herself earlier that no matter what, she would not surrender and be seen crying for a man who had abandoned her. As the saying went, "*Moipolai ga llelwi sello sa gagwe ke moropa*" – he who kills himself does not deserve anyone's tears but the beating of a drum. They should be dancing, then, she thought.

Ama sat on the mattress laid down on the floor against the wall. She was covered in a light black blanket, assuming her widowed status. All eyes were on her, sympathetic in their stares. It was unfathomable, what had happened to her, they seemed to say, abandoned at such a young age. Their sad thoughts mingled in the air above Ama: stories similar to hers spoken, recounts of women marrying their dead fiancés. There were whispers of Ama being cursed, of never being able to have another man; all the men she'd get involved with after this would die, they whispered. Sorrowful clucks of the tongue sounded here and there.

Thabo's mother was sitting next to her. From time to time, the old woman would place her hand on Ama's shoulder, letting it linger. To Ama it felt like a branding iron, reinforcing everything the faces surrounding her were saying.

"He'll arrive any minute now." The words reached Ama in the semi-darkness of the candlelight. She didn't know what time it was, but she knew she'd been sitting on the mattress for a long time. Like a bride waiting for her groom to unveil her to the world, she had been waiting.

"He's outside. The men will carry him in."

The hand of the old woman sitting next to her swiftly returned. Ama flinched.

"My son is finally home," Thabo's mother hand tensed, gripping Ama's shoulder. From outside, Ama could hear the shuffling of feet weighed down by their burden. Their slow tread sounded like a legion of men defeated in battle.

A melancholy voice rent the air in a song of lament. The singer went on, her voice accepting the solemnity and sadness Thabo's arrival had brought. Soon other voices joined her song, and people started pushing up off the floor. Forming a line, they filed out of the dimly lit room to go and pay their last respects to Thabo. Ama was the last to be pulled from the mattress. Her black-swathed body was guided gently to where Thabo's mother, father and brother stood, alongside Thabo's coffin. The parent's faces were bleak and tearful, but Thabo's brother appeared devoid of any emotion.

Ama was called forward. The coffin was made of fine mahogany. It gleamed, catching light in random places. When she stepped closer, her shadow darkened the shiny surface, sending a shiver through her. Ama looked in on him. He appeared serene. Perfect, Ama thought. For a moment, seeing him lying there, she felt a strange peace, the anger and torment receded.

"Sleep well, my love," she silently said to him. She wanted to kiss him, but she couldn't. Not with everyone watching her.

"Come," Ama heard Pamela gently say. She realised she had been standing there crying silently. She let Pamela guide her out of the room, and back to the mattress. Pamela handed her a tissue to wipe her face.

"Is your arm better? I see you're not wearing your sling," she said, sniffing.

"Yes, it wasn't broken, you know." Pamela said, looking away.

"Where is Mandla?"

"He's out there somewhere."

"Thank him for me, will you?" Ama gave Pamela a weak smile.

"Sure."

"We would have been married a week tomorrow."

"I know." Pamela took Ama's hand.

"You know, I've never asked anyone this question, not even God," Ama said looking past Pamela into the dark room.

"What, Ama?"

"Why me, Pam? Why did this happen? And why me?"

"I don't know, Ama," Pamela said. "I wish I did."

"I couldn't cry at all in the beginning." Ama wiped at her face. "But now I can't seem to stop."

"Maybe you shouldn't try to stop yourself. Thabo does deserve your tears," Pamela said, tightening her grip on Ama's hand.

"No, he doesn't. Not the way he left me, he doesn't," she said, crying harder.

"Oh Ama!" Pamela drew her friend to her, letting her cry. Neither heard the door open.

"Oh, baby." Matlakala walked in, Beauty following behind her. She hurried to Ama's side. "Beauty, bring her something to drink," she said. "Tea with a lot of sugar." She sat down in front of Ama.

"I can't imagine how you feel, Ama, but I know you are strong, and that with time you will get through this."

"I believe that too," Pamela said.

"The next thing you're going to say is that life is a circle. And I must take the good with the bad," Ama said. Seeing the look on their faces, she added, "Lighten up guys, I meant it as a joke."

"That wasn't funny," Pamela said, giving Ama a smile.

"We should plan a trip after everything goes back to normal. I feel like I haven't done anything fun in a long time" Ama said.

"That's a good idea" Matlakala said "I would love a holiday."

"We could go to Zanzibar. I saw pictures. It's really beautiful there."

"Sorry, ladies," Beauty interrupted from the doorway, a mug of steaming tea in her hand, "but we need to go. Thabo's family has asked everybody to gather outside."

"Why, what is happening out there?" Ama asked anxiously.

"I'm sure it's nothing. They probably just want to say a prayer with everyone." Pamela got to her feet, helping up Ama.

"Actually Ama is supposed to stay here," Beauty said with a grimace. "They said so."

After her words there was a questioning silence, each of them afraid to ask why.

"It's not a big deal. We'll find you here once we hear what they have to say," Pamela said.

"I better give you this before it gets cold." Beauty handed Ama the tea.

"Thanks, Beauty. Could you please tell my brother to come and see me."

"Sure," Beauty said, sympathy etched in her voice.

Alone, Ama sipped slowly her tea. From outside, she heard the sad voice of the singer again. They were indeed in prayer, and she was not invited. She wished she could be there. Next, Thabo's eulogy would be read. Suddenly Ama wanted to speak to him. She wanted to ask him why he had left her behind. She thought of the note. Those were his last thoughts to her. What had he said? If only she could go home and read it now. For a moment she considered leaving.

"You wanted to see me, sis?" Jeffrey walked in.

"Yes, I was feeling lonely," Ama said. "Why have I been left here alone?"

Jeffrey sat down next to her. "There's nothing to worry about, sis. You didn't do anything wrong." His voice was soft but adamant. "Actually I'm glad you called me in here. Thabo's uncle was getting to me out there." He faked joviality.

"Oh?"

"Yeah, I think he's lost it a bit."

"What do you mean?" Ama asked.

"It's nothing to worry about. He'll be fine by tomorrow."

"That's the second time you've told me not worry. Is something wrong?"

"Nothing's wrong, Ama. Tomorrow we'll bury Thabo and everything will be fine." Ama looked at her brother. She knew he was not telling the truth, but suddenly felt overcome by exhaustion. Whatever it was, she would find out soon enough. She sat back, closing her eyes and letting the sorrowful music wash over her.

Jeffrey sat back next to her, sighing.

"Everything will be fine," he repeated.

Chapter 8

It was done. Thabo was buried, and the mourners had dispersed, leaving Ama to get on with her life, for better or for worse.

The first thing she planned to do was go back to work. The hospital needed her now; they were short-staffed. And Ama needed things to go back to normal as soon as possible.

She glanced at her friends, who had been keeping her company while she waited outside Thabo's house for the last of the mourners to leave.

"Ama," she heard a man's voice, soft and slightly hesitant.

"Yes?" She looked up.

"I am Lazaro, Thabo's brother …"

"Yes?"

"I've been sent to bring you inside."

"Sent by whom, Mr Maboa?" Beauty quickly asked. "What is this about?"

"Beauty …" Pamela said, eyeing Thabo's brother cautiously. The man just stood there blank faced, as though he did not understand what was happening. There were rumours that something was wrong with Thabo's brother. Looking at him now, it was clear that something was the matter. He stood there, unmoving, his eyes fixed on Ama's face.

"You must come with me," he said with such finality that Ama was taken aback.

She got to her feet, and without a word followed him, leaving her friends looking on in surprise.

On entering the house, she found the front room filled with people, every chair occupied.

"Thank you, Lazaro, for bringing her." His father extended his hands towards Ama in welcome. The old man seemed happy to see her. Lazaro nodded stiffly, and sat down on a wooden chair close by.

"Ama, please sit." Lazaro's father guided her to the chair next to his son. She hadn't noticed Jeffrey when she'd first come in. His body was tense, and there was something in his eyes, Ama couldn't fathom. She wished she could ask him what was happening. Her eyes scanned the room: gathered there were the people who'd been at the lobola negotiations and a man she hadn't seen before, wearing an expensive looking black suit.

"Brother, I think you can take it from here." Mr Maboa turned to the man next to him, who stood up and began speaking.

"As Thabo's uncle, I represent the Maboa family. Sad circumstances bring us to this gathering. I wish we were not here today for this reason, but what must be done must be done." A few heads nodded, prompting him to continue.

"Before my nephew died, he was in the process of getting married. No, let me put that correctly. When Thabo died, he was already married. In our tradition, paying lobola and holding the amalgamating ceremony the families and ancestors is viewed as a ritual that connects two people in marriage. Therefore, Mr and Mrs Maboa now have a daughter that they have to take care of, as their son Thabo is no longer here to do his duty. The best way they can do this, to the best of their ability, is to offer their bride to their son, Lazaro," he said, pointing to Lazaro.

Stunned, Ama jumped to her feet. "What? You cannot be serious!" Ama faced the crowded room, anger coursing through her body. They looked back at her, their faces stern. "Thabo is dead, he killed himself. He did that all on his own. You can't expect Lazaro to be his brother's keeper. I don't need anybody to take care of me!"

"We believe you don't know what you need at this time."

"And you do?"

"Yes, that's the reason why this decision has been taken on your behalf."

"I'm not a child that you can control."

"You must understand, we're not trying to control you. We're only doing this for your own good. You only have to accept it. There is no use fighting."

"What?" Ama asked incredulous, "I don't have a choice in this?" Ama turned around, searching their faces. They actually believed she had no choice.

"No!" she cried.

"Ama," Jeffrey crossed the room to his sister.

"What, Jeffrey? Did you know about his?" she screamed out her words.

"Ama, please. Listen to what they have to say." Jeffrey looked defeated.

"You're not telling me that you agree with this insane idea?"

Jeffrey did not answer.

She stared at him, disbelief turning to horror. "Jeffrey?" she grabbed his arms, shaking them. "Surely you don't expect me to sit here while they trade me off from one dead brother to another?" Ama could feel panic rising in her breast.

"This is not a trade-off, daughter," Thabo's uncle intervened, his voice soft but firm. "It is the only way the Maboa family can ensure that you're taken care of properly."

Ama took a few deep breaths to steady herself. This was so ridiculous, she wondered momentarily if she was having a nightmare. "First of all, I'm not your daughter. Secondly, I'm a grown woman. I can take care of myself! I am not some possession to be passed around! For goodness sake, this is the twenty-first century!"

"Ama!" Her face tear-stained, Thabo's mother stepped forward. "Please Ama, you must let us do this for you. After what's happened, this is the only way we can make it up to you."

Ama felt frantic. "But, Mme, you don't have to make up for anything! Don't you understand? Have you gone mad?" She pleaded, looking around the room for someone who was on her side, who could see sense, and wishing that this really was just a nightmare.

"Shhh, Ama, please, calm down. I can understand that you are upset. I know our customs might seem strange to you, and it might be difficult for you to accept this now. You are still grieving. But in time you will see that Lazaro is a good man, and I know that he will help you heal. Please, just listen to my brother." Mma Maboa held on to Ama's hands.

"No!" Ama wrenched her hands away. "I will not listen to any more of this! This is madness!"

She turned to walk out of the room.

"Ama, you will listen to what we have to say." Thabo's uncle stepped in front of her. "Please, sit down."

Looking at his face, Ama wavered. She would not have put it past him to forcibly restrain her. Shaken, she sat down again.

Thabo's uncle turned to the man in the suit.

"This is Jacob Madi, Thabo's lawyer. He is here to read us Thabo's will."

Thabo's uncle ushered the man to the front of the room. Sitting down, he seemed to lose some of his composure, and he rubbed at his temples, visibly strained.

The lawyer took out a sheath of papers from his briefcase, and began to read. Ama sat mutely, as if in a trance, the voice of the lawyer drifting in and out of her consciousness. At one point she became aware of Lazaro, who still had said nothing. What on earth was he thinking? Surely he had something to say about all this? Ama felt her anger rising.

The lawyer had finished speaking. Ama had taken in little of what he said. She couldn't stop thinking of Thabo's family's wish that Ama should be cared for by his brother.

"Come, Ama," she heard Jeffrey say. "Let's go home. We can sort out things there."

"Sort things out?" she spat at him.

"Please, Ama. We'll talk about this at home. Let's just leave." Ama looked at him for a long while. She had never felt more betrayed.

"So, what, are you just going to sell off your sister? My husband didn't love me enough to stay alive, and I am being punished! Now you want me to spend the rest of my life with someone who is mentally unstable, probably because his family doesn't know what else to do with him!" Ama felt close to hysterical. Gasps of shock met her outburst, but nobody challenged her.

"That's enough, Ama!" Jeffrey took her arm and dragged her towards the door and outside to his car.

On the ride home, they didn't speak, and as soon as they arrived, Ama went straight into her room, locking the door behind her.

Sitting on the edge of her bed, she picked up Thabo's letter, as she had so many times since the day he had died. It was still sealed. She turned it around in her hands, trying to work up the courage to open it.

Chapter 9

The ladies watched Ama's sudden disappearance to her room. She hadn't spoken a word, but they could feel the tension.

Beauty looked at Jeffrey. Something was wrong. She'd never seen him like this.

"What's the matter?" Beauty asked. No one answered. Jeffrey went to his room. She followed him there.

"Do you want to talk about it?"

"I want to be alone. I think you should go." Beauty gasped, pained at his rejection. She searched his face to see if he'd meant what he said. But he said nothing, and only turned away from her. Silently, she walked out of his room.

After leaving Ama's house, Beauty could not face going home. Instead, she carried on walking, past her road, finding her way to the park she and Jeffrey had gone to so many times. She sat on their bench, watching the passersby and going over their encounter in her mind.

Oh! She was a fool. Why had she thought this time would be different? She had even put her mother at risk of being exposed.

"I have to end this!" Beauty's hands covered her face. "But do I really want to end it?" Pamela had said it that very afternoon: "Whatever you choose, you lose." But she had to make a decision. Although she knew the decision had already been made for her. Jeffrey had had enough.

Late afternoon had turned to evening, and a mist had risen, blurring the light of the lampposts dotted around the park.

Beauty began to walk home, her head bowed and her arms wrapped around her chest. There were still people in the park. Now and then she caught sound of laughter or someone calling to a dog. She walked on quicker, her heels echoing on the stoned pathway. She rounded a bend and almost collided into a couple. For a moment, her heart pulled at the sight of their embrace.

"Sorry, I didn't see you there," she mumbled.

"It's fine." Something about the man's voice stopped her.

She turned to look at him. The mist had grown thicker, and his face was partially obscured by the woman's arm around his neck. But he looked familiar.

She hesitated before carrying on.

All the way home, it bothered her. Where had she heard that voice before?

After putting the children to bed, Pamela lingered in the kitchen, putting away the last of the dishes. Mandla was scaring her again. He'd gone to their room straight after supper. She hoped he had would be asleep by the time she was finished. She didn't want to face him tonight. She feared what he might do or say.

She thought back to their conversation the day of Thabo's death, shuddering as she recalled his hateful words about Thabo's suicide. Pamela didn't know what to make of his words. Part of her didn't want to think about it, but what he had said bothered her. There had been something disturbing about his reaction, beyond his usual callousness. Was there something Mandla knew? And should she tell someone? What if there was more to Thabo's death than they knew? She shook her head, willing the thoughts to go away. That would mean having to repeat the conversation with Mandla, and she trembled at the thought of what he might do if he found out she was interfering.

It was getting late, and Pamela had run out of things to tidy in her already immaculate house. She would have to go to bed. Mercifully, Mandla was asleep. Pamela changed quickly, keeping her movements to the minimum so that she wouldn't make any noise. Sliding into bed, she waited for any sign of disturbing him. When he didn't move, she closed her eyes and hoped for sleep to come quickly.

The cellphone droned on and on. From a deep sleep, Matlakala heard it, like the irritating buzz of a mosquito. She reached for it, glancing at the time. It was 4 am. Who could be calling her at this hour? She looked to her side. Joe wasn't there. Pain stabbed her heart. Why do I put up with this, she asked herself for the hundredth time, pushing the answer button.

"Is Joe there?"

It was a woman.

"Who is this?" Matlakala sat up, feeling suddenly ill.

"Never mind who I am. What's important is that you can't give the phone to your so-called boyfriend. Do you know why?"

Matlakala already knew the answer. She could hear it in the other woman's voice. "Because he's right here next to me, sleeping. Isn't he gorgeous, when he's asleep? He looks like a boy." The woman laughed. She sounded drunk, or high.

"Anyway, enjoy the rest of your night, or what's left of it anyway." Then the line went dead. Matlakala slowly put down her phone.

She had known Joe was unfaithful, but what man wasn't? It was one of those things that a woman is aware of, but is comforted by the fact that at least her man doesn't let her know about it. As long as he comes back to me, right? Now where was he? Matlakala felt tears welling. All she wanted was to make it work. But what would it take? How long would she have to wait for the life she wanted?

"God, I am not asking for much!" Matlakala felt like screaming. How had she become so helpless? She stared into space, her mind racing. This could not go on. For the first time, she admitted to herself: she had to rid herself of Joe. The thought scared her, and she tried to shove it to wherever it came from, but it wouldn't go away. Enough! A voice in her head cried out. You have to do something! But what?

There was no point trying to go back to sleep. She got up and went to switch on her computer. She might as well get something done while she was awake. As for Joe, she'd come to a decision soon enough.

Chapter 10

A month had passed, and things had returned to some degree of normalcy for the four women. Joe had shown up at her house three days later, without any explanation, and as usual Matlakala had not asked for any.

Pamela had returned to work, and Mandla was keeping his distance, for the moment. Sizwe seemed to have forgiven her, and her wounds had healed. She knew it would not last, but for now she was content.

Beauty had not seen Jeffrey since the day he'd rejected her. She felt hurt, but it was a feeling so familiar, it was almost comforting. And she told herself it was better to accept that things were over. That way he couldn't hurt her any more.

Ama had been living in a state of limbo. For the past few weeks life had gone on as if nothing had happened, but tomorrow all that would change, when she entered into the home of her dead husband's brother, her keeper. For weeks she had argued with Thabo's family, but no one seemed to care what she thought or what she felt. Finally she had given in: eventually they would have to see that this was unnecessary. And insane. What kind of tradition meant that a woman should be stripped of her rights, identity and independence? The way Ama saw it, the Maboa family were using her to retain their family name, as Thabo had left her his entire estate. She wondered what he would have thought about this. He barely had a chance to settle in his grave and his would-have-been wife was being given to another man.

The night before, Ama had walked into the kitchen to find Jeffrey slumped at the table, his head resting in his hands. She had never seem him look so sad, not even after her parents died, and her heart had gone out to him, but she wouldn't allow her feelings to show, not when her anger was still so fresh.

"You'd think you were the one being parcelled off to some crazed substitute husband," she said.

Jeffrey looked up at her, and she could see that his eyes were swollen and bloodshot. "Just remember, Ama, Lazaro is not your husband. You don't have to do anything with him. He's just there to take care of you."

"Does this arrangement have a manual? It seems everyone knows the rules except me."

Jeffrey held out his hands, defeated. "I just want you to know that you don't have to do anything you don't want to do."

"Really?" Ama laughed bitterly.

Now, the day of departure had arrived, and she stood in her living room, alongside her suitcases, waiting for Jeffrey to carry them out to the car.

She looked around the room. This was the only home she knew. Even after her parents' death, the house had still felt like home, with all the memories it held of her parents and their childhood. Ama closed her eyes, thinking of her mother and father. A gust of wind blew through the window, softly brushing her skin, and a strange calm came over her. She sank into it, forgetting everything else.

"Are you ready?" Jeffrey asked from the doorway. She had not heard him come in.

"There's no carrying me down the aisle, is there?" Ama said. Jeffrey looked at her for a while, and then bent to lift her suitcases, his movements slow and heavy. Ama could see he was hurting for her. But she could not help feeling betrayed.

"Are you ready?" he asked again.

"No, I'm still waiting for my friends to come, and then we can go. You don't mind if they come, do you?"

He shook his head. Ama wondered if they would ever be close again.

"Oh, before I forget …" She reached out a hand to her dressing table, picking up Thabo's suicide note.

Jeffrey said nothing as she put it carefully into her case.

Outside, she turned to her brother. "Have you spoken to Beauty yet?"

"No, I haven't. Why?"

Ignoring his question, Ama said, "You know, Jeffrey, any fool can see you love her, or you wouldn't be putting up with her. Why don't you tell her how you feel?"

"Because …" Jeffrey frowned. "Because she's not ready to know how I feel."

"If you wait for her to be ready, it might be too late."

Matlakala's car pulled up, and Ama's friends got out.

Pamela walked over to Ama and squeezed her hand.

"Okay, Ama, we're here," she said simply.

It was already afternoon when they made their way to Ama's new home. Ama watched in panic as they turned onto Braamfisher Road. This was the home that Thabo had bought for them. She'd seen the house once. And now she was going to see it without him. Getting out of the car, she stood for a moment on the pavement, unsure of her next move. The house was a double-storey cream building with balconies and a long driveway that stretched from the gate to the double-door garage. Shrubbery and flowers dotted open and unpaved spaces.

Standing in front of it, Ama felt overwhelmed. This should have been hers and Thabo's new home. She should be arriving here as Mrs Thabo Maboa, not to do this disgraceful thing – what Thabo's family called "fixing things".

"I can't do this," Ama said.

"It's okay, Ama. We'll stay overnight with you." Pamela looked at Matlakala and Beauty for their agreement. They nodded.

"What about Lazaro, won't he mind?" Ama asked, grimacing at her own words. There it was, she thought. The moment she stepped into that house she would be losing her freedom. She was becoming the property of a man she hardly knew, no matter what anyone said. Ama cast her eyes around apprehensively. Would she have felt this way about Thabo? Of course not: she had loved him. It had taken his death for her to realise how much.

"Don't worry, I'll speak to him," Jeffrey said. "Let's go in, Lazaro is probably waiting for us." He could feel Beauty's stare on him, and he avoided her accusing eyes. They had hardly spoken on the way.

The five walked into the house, wrapped in a mournful silence, as though Thabo had died all over again. The women walked through the rooms, taking in the tasteful décor, each imagining the life that Thabo and Ama might have shared there.

Lazaro was waiting in the hallway. He wasn't alone. Thabo's uncle was there too. He was the only person who looked happy. Well, he had got what he wanted, Ama thought.

"We're glad you made it, daughter," he said. "Mr and Mrs Maboa have sent their regret at not being here to welcome you to your new home." Lazaro's uncle seemed immune to the awkwardness of the situation.

"I understand. I'm sure this place must make them think of Thabo." Ama looked around her.

"Yes, well," he said, momentarily taken aback, before clearing his throat.

"Everybody, please, make yourself comfortable. This is your home, Ama." He sat down on one of the sofas, and the rest followed suit. Ama looked at Lazaro, who had taken a seat across from her. As usual, he had the appearance of a detached observer. How was it possible that he could be so unmoved, when his whole life was being decided for him? Did he really not care? Was it true that he was mentally disturbed? Well, she would soon find out.

Ama got up and walked over to her luggage. There she opened one of the large cases and brought out her quilt. A gasp escaped Matlakala's lips. Pamela looked shocked, and Beauty pursed her lips together tightly, as if fighting back her words.

Ama knew what this quilt represented to the women. It was their love for each other, stitched together to form a symbol of their love and a blessing for the union of love between Ama and Thabo. For a moment, she clutched it to her breast, before carrying it over to the stunned group.

"Lazaro," she said his name breathlessly.

Lazaro blinked, as though waking from sleep. His expression did not change, but his eyes bore into Ama's.

"What you see here was supposed to have belonged to your brother. It was my wedding gift to him. But since you're in some way to be your brother's keeper, I'll give this to you." She handed over the quilt and went back to her chair.

"Thank you," he said, his eyes still fixed on her. With tears in her eyes, Ama stared back. She had been prepared for him to refuse it, to deny the position his brother's death had put him in, but he hadn't – Lazaro had received the quilt, as simply as he could. This made her sadder than ever. With Thabo, the quilt would have been an exotic landscape beneath which they explored each other's bodies. It would have held their secrets and cocooned their love, and bred them memories. The tears that had been hovering spilled over, dragging forth a sound of sorrow from deep within her.

"Ama, it's okay." Pamela was quick to place a hand on her shoulder. Matlakala looked around uncomfortably. Jeffrey, his tears brimming at his own eyelashes, looked on the verge of breaking down. Matlakala nudged Beauty in the ribs.

"I'm dying to see the rest of the house," Beauty said with a fake smile. "Ama, maybe you could show us around?"

"Oh, yes." Ama wiped her eyes and got up.

Jeffrey sent Beauty a grateful smile. "We can start in the kitchen. Excuse us."

Lazaro's uncle blinked several times, nodded, and then looked away.

The four ladies made their way to the direction of the kitchen.

"I was thinking of going back to work tomorrow," Ama said. "I don't think I can bear being idle for another day."

The other three women looked at each other.

"That's understandable," Pamela said, picking and examining a porcelain vase, but maybe you should give yourself some time to settle in here first."

"I'm not the first woman to become a widow, you know. I need to move on!"

"Yes, that's true," Matlakala said gently, "but you need to be strong for your patients. How can you do that while you are not feeling strong yourself?"

"Matlakala is right, Ama. Just take a few more days off. The hospital will understand, I'm sure."

"No one asked you, Beauty," Ama couldn't hold back the rage that had been building any longer. "And don't act like you feel anything for me, Miss Nothing-can-touch-me. I don't want your fake sympathy – we both know you don't care."

"Ama, not now," Pamela tried to soothe the situation.

"When then, Pam? When is it ever the right time to say anything, do anything? Can't you see? Days go by, and I do nothing. We do nothing!" She paced the room, feeling the anger burning her skin. She felt close to lashing out at one of the women.

Beauty stood with her arms on her hips. "You know what, I can do without this," she said. "I'm leaving."

"Fine, Beauty, you do that! Like you always do. Whenever there's a little bit of heat, you leave. Just go, and leave us all in peace. You bring out the worst in me, anyway," Ama shouted, before collapsing on a barstool and breaking down in tears.

"Ama, that's not fair. Beauty is here because of you," Matlakala said.

"Matlakala." Pamela softly shook her head. She poured water into a cup and passed it to Ama.

"Whose side are you on, anyway?" Matlakala's voice rose in pitch.

"It's not about sides," Pamela said.

Ama's weeping grew louder.

"What the hell!" Jeffrey burst into the kitchen. "What's happening in here? We can hear you ladies all the way from the sitting room. Ama, are you okay?"

"I'm fine," Ama said, casting a guilty look at Beauty, who was standing near the door looking uncomfortable.

Ama walked over to the sink and splashed some cold water on her face. Why had she lashed out at Beauty like that? This situation had turned her into a crazy woman.

"Are you alright, daughter?" It was Lazaro's uncle. Ama could hear the discomfort in his voice. Would he mention her behaviour to her in-laws?

"I'm fine now," Ama said, looking in irritation at the people around her. How dare they treat her as if she were mad, when they had forced her into this insane set-up? "I was going to prepare some coffee," she said, willing her voice to stay calm. "Would you like some?"

"Oh, no," Lazaro's uncle said. "I think it's time I left you young people to your house. I'll come for coffee another time." He left the kitchen, Lazaro meekly following behind.

Ama wanted to scream at the whole world. But what was the use? Essentially, she had accepted this situation. And now she had to deal with it.

"Coffee anyone?" she repeated. She began opening cupboards.

That evening passed surprisingly peacefully. Beauty had left with Jeffrey, assuring Ama that she wasn't angry, just tired. The other three had retired to Ama's room. It had been a long time since Ama had spent some time with her friends. Sitting in her new bedroom, the door firmly shut, she felt safe.

"It's not so bad here," Matlakala said, lying back on Ama's bed and stretching.

"I was just thinking the same thing." Pamela said smoothing the blanket on her lap. They seemed to recede into their thoughts pondering whatever bothered their minds.

"Ama, why are you so angry with Beauty?" Matlakala asked.

"I'm not ..."

"You could have fooled me. Sometimes I wonder why you stay friends with her."

"Matlakala, I don't think we should be speaking about this now," Pamela said.

"I'm not arguing, Pam. I just want to know what it is about Beauty that bothers Ama so much. I know she's not the most sensitive person alive, but still ..."

Ama interjected. "Doesn't it bother you the way she picks on you all the time?"

"Well, she usually has a point."

"Are you talking about Joe?"

Matlakala sighed. "Look, this isn't about me. All I'm saying is that if you avoid a situation long enough, it comes for you."

Ama looked at her friend. When had it started? She had always been so close to Beauty.

"I think it started when she and Jeffrey got together," she said.

"I always thought it had something to do with Jeffrey." Matlakala nodded.

"Were you angry that they started seeing each other?" Pamela asked.

"No, it's not that. Jeffrey could have dated anyone, and I wouldn't have minded. But have you noticed the way Beauty lives her life? It's as if she doesn't have a care in the world. Nothing seems to touch her, but when my brother noticed her, she changed. Even though she acted like she didn't want him, I could tell she loved him."

"You envy her?" Matlakala said.

"It's not that. It's hard to explain. Sometimes I feel like she's laughing behind our backs. Bad things have happened to you, Pamela, and to me, and we have carried on. But with Beauty, it's like she doesn't want to be here. I don't even know why, but it bothers me. And I'm tired of the way she treats people, as if she expects us all to act as unfeeling as her. I don't know why you defend her."

"I'm not. But Beauty is Beauty, and at the end of the day she's our friend. And if she didn't want to be here for you, she wouldn't have come, Ama."

"Maybe." Ama felt too tired to argue any more. Her husband was dead, and she was stuck with a strange man – the last thing she needed was to fall out with her friends.

"So, what do you know about Lazaro?" Pamela asked tentatively, changing the topic.

"Not much. He barely speaks."

"You know that he has no rights over you, don't you?"

"It depends what you mean by rights."

"Well, when a man dies and a woman is widowed, she is given a choice as to whether she wants someone to continue on her husband's behalf. The man she chooses is given the responsibilities of the deceased. He visits sometimes to make sure that the household continues. But in your case, Lazaro has no rights, because you didn't choose him. In fact you didn't want anyone to take care of you. The Maboa family gave him to you. And they had no right to do that." Ama looked carefully at Pamela. "Are you saying this means I can go home and live my own life?" Ama felt a spark of hope flickering. "Why didn't you tell me this sooner, Pam?"

"Well, it's not that simple. I don't want you to get your hopes up, darling." Pamela looked worried.

"Why not?" Ama's voice rose.

"Well, think about Thabo," Pamela said. At the mention of his name Matlakala drew a breath, glancing nervously at Ama.

"What does he have to do with it?" Ama said.

"Everything, Ama." Pamela's voice trembled. "He's the reason you're here."

"But that doesn't mean I have to be here. He chose his path, and I should be entitled to choose my own."

Tears poured down Pamela's cheeks. "Maybe this is your path, Ama."

Chapter 11

Matlakala stretched lightly as she walked towards the kitchen. She'd been sent to make some tea and a large cup of coffee for Ama. Matlakala wondered how Ama managed to sleep, with all the caffeine she drank.

The house was beautiful, Matlakala thought, looking around her. It was a shame that Ama wouldn't be able to appreciate it. Why was it that nothing good seemed to happen to them? Matlakala's life seemed to be getting harder every day. All she had ever wanted was to find a man who loved her, to share her life. She couldn't remember the last time she had laughed with Joe. He was alive, and yet here she was mourning him like he was dead. Matlakala switched on the kettle. Maybe she was finally ready to move forward. The thought lifted her spirits slightly.

"Hello."

She turned to find Lazaro standing behind her.

"I'm making tea, would you like some?"

"No, thank you." An awkward silence ensued as he stared at her. She couldn't think of a single thing to say to him.

The kettle hissed behind her. He was a strange man, she thought to herself.

At the sink, Lazaro was rinsing a few brushes sprinkled with paint.

"Are you a painter?" she asked, curious.

"I wouldn't say that … I paint from time to time."

"You don't look like a painter," Matlakala said without thinking.

"Well, a lot of people don't look like they can do anything."

"Yes, that's true. But some people like to pretend."

"What purpose would that serve?"

Matlakala wondered about the rumours that she had heard. Something told her that they couldn't be true. He seemed intelligent.

"Well, to impress others, I suppose." Lazaro turned away, as if disappointed with Matlakala's answer. Well, Matlakala thought, annoyed at his rudeness, maybe it was true that he lacked social skills. She poured hot water into a tea pot. She was about to leave when Lazaro's voice stopped her.

"A person never looks like anything other than who they are. It is the observer who decides what he or she should be. And I believe that is seldom what that person is." He finished washing his brushes and started to wipe them quietly. Flustered, Matlakala looked at him. Although strange, his words made sense to her.

"How can you do it?" Matlakala asked, wide eyed.

"Do what?"

"Sacrifice your own life to live with your brother's widow. I mean, you must have ideas of your own, dreams." Suddenly, Matlakala found that she wanted to know what drove this man.

"Don't we all have to make sacrifices, in one way or another?"

"Maybe, but yours seem extreme, don't you think? I mean, wouldn't you like to be free to marry the woman you want?"

"I'm not married to Ama. As for whether what I'm doing is extreme, well maybe. But so is what Thabo did. And that is why I have to do this."

"You really are different, aren't you?"

"Not different, just simple. I think your water is getting cold, by the way."

"Why do you think Thabo killed himself?" Matlakala immediately regretted the question. Where was her filter? Now was the time to retreat with the coffee and tea.

"I'm sorry; it's none of my business." She picked up her tray and hurried out of the kitchen, leaving.

Lazaro returned to his brushes. She wondered what it would be like living with someone like him. Perhaps they would all be better off alone, she sighed.

Beauty could not get Ama's words out of her mind. Ama was one of the few people who could get to Beauty, threatening to expose her don't-care attitude. She needed a break, Beauty decided, a respite from everything, including Ama. Beauty figured Ama's attitude had something to do with Jeffrey. But if she had a problem with their relationship, she should come out and say it!

Beauty sighed, remembering Ama's comment about her leaving. Maybe she was right. But she had to get away. She would find some place in the middle of nowhere, with no cellphone reception and where no one would bother her. Calling out goodnight to her mother, Beauty felt a twinge of guilt at the thought of leaving her alone. Before she left she would buy her mother something to read. She lay back, and her thoughts drifted to Jeffrey and their conversation on the ride home.

"I'm sorry my sister spoke to you the way she did. She's under a lot of strain."

"I understand, Jeffrey. You don't have to apologise." Beauty had not expected this.

"You remember when I said we needed to talk?" he said.

"Yes. But we don't have to do this now. It's been a long day," she said, wondering if he'd forgotten his recent rejection of her. She didn't want to talk about this.

"I know, but there is something I want to say."

"Yes?" Beauty swallowed, fearing his words.

"Do you see that you are taking us backwards?" Beauty could hear the disappointment in his voice. He sounded so defeated that she couldn't say what she wanted to say.

"Jeffrey, I know. But let's not talk about this right now, not yet."

"Okay, I know it's been a hard day. But promise me we will talk about it soon?"

"Okay."

Now, lying in her bed, she decided that she could not keep her promise. When she came back, she would tell him it was over. It was the only way. Beauty stared at the ceiling, waiting for night to finish its stroll across the sky and for morning to come. When she came back, she would be strong again, ready for anything, she hoped.

Chapter 12

The next day, Ama woke to a world turned upside down. The peace and camaraderie of the previous night was now gone, replaced by cold reality. Mechanically, she made her way to the kitchen. Her head hurt from the jumble of thoughts and emotions. Lazaro entered the kitchen then, helping himself to coffee from the percolator.

She mumbled a greeting. All she could focus on right now was the hot sweetened taste of coffee.

At least she was not one for the bottle: she would have been a few down by now, to dull her mind.

She was so tired of the endless cycle of thoughts that never seemed to lead to any solution. She had to find something to do. You could play wife: uncalled for words popped into her head.

No, that was the last thing she'd ever do. Her husband was dead. The thought brought fresh tears to her eyes. Thabo was gone. Sniffing, Ama knew she had to do something to get her life back. She picked up her phone and called the hospital, asking to speak to Matron Makgoba.

The woman sounded surprised. "Ama! How is everything going?"

"Things are fine, thanks matron. Actually I think I am ready to come back. I'd like to come on duty tomorrow morning."

"Why? You still have a few days left."

"I just need to do something with my time," she said, feeling desperate.

"Ama …"

"Really, I'm fine. I'm just going a bit crazy with nothing to do!"

"Okay, fine. Come in tomorrow, and we'll see how it goes."

"Thank you."

Ama hung up the phone, feeling like she had taken a step in the right direction. The tension that was within her eased and she felt her shoulders relaxing.

Pamela's morning had also turned out better than she'd expected. She had pushed her worries to the back of her mind, turned on her charm and boarded her tour bus, smiling at the faces eagerly waiting to listen to her, to have her show them the beauty in Soweto. They listened attentively as the bus began the journey through the winding streets, while she spoke about Soweto's people, history and legacy. It gave her pleasure, watching the strangers soak up the sights and stories, living experiences that would become treasured memories. Pamela sometimes wished she saw the township, the monuments and historical landmarks through their eyes, for the first time.

For the rest of the day, Pamela had carried the joy and gratitude of the tourists with her. For a change, she felt a sense of possibility, of freedom. The feelings stayed with her when her children arrived home, and as she went about her household chores, careful not to rush anything. She wanted to hold on to this serenity. But in the back of her mind, she knew it would not last. Mandla would come home, and everything she'd been feeling would fade.

But night fell, and Mandla had not returned. She began to feel apprehensive, anticipating the moment he returned. Surely it will be any minute now, Pamela thought. She wondered what he would say when he saw her. Maybe nothing – who was she kidding? She knew he didn't like it when she slept away from home; he was so suspicious of her. But, last night she had wanted to help her friend and gone against his rules. Pamela took another breath. It hadn't bothered her last night; in fact she hadn't thought about it all day long, until now.

"If you carrying on panting like that, you might pass out," Mandla said, his mouth close to her ear. Pamela's eyes grew huge. She could feel her chest constrict, making breathing difficult. She tried to compose herself. "Ah," she began, breathlessly. "I was doing some breathing exercises."

"Really?" he asked, his tone mocking.

"Yes," she said, stepping away from him. "It relaxes me."

"Oh," he said, sounding bored suddenly. "Here. Phone for you." He handed her the receiver. Pamela looked questioningly at him. She hadn't heard the phone ring or him coming through the door.

"It's your friend, Ama. Sounds like something's wrong again. She's a bit of a basket case, isn't she?" He handed Pamela the phone and walked off.

"Thank God," Ama said. "I thought that husband of yours was playing games with me, putting me on hold for nothing."

"No, never mind him. How has your day been?"

"Okay. I'm going back to work tomorrow, which is a relief. Finally I'll have something to do other than sit here and stare at the walls."

"Where is Lazaro? He hasn't disappeared, has he?" Pamela watched as Mandla walked back into the sitting room. But he seemed to be ignoring her. Pamela wondered why.

"No, he's somewhere in the house. But I've been in my room all day."

"Have you eaten something? You should eat, you know. You need to keep strong." It was weird that she wanted Mandla's attention, Pamela thought, as her eyes watched him walking around the sitting room.

"I know. I'll eat something later. But I'm not hungry now. Anyway, how are you?"

"I'm fine, can't complain." What was wrong with her? Did she want him to turn on her? It was a blessing he wasn't paying her any attention.

"Pam, I don't mean to pry, but Mandla sounded … I don't know how to put this, but it was weird. Is everything okay?"

"Yes, everything is fine."

"Are you sure?" Ama asked.

"Yes, I'm sure? He's fine, I'm fine."

"Okay, don't get annoyed. I just got the feeling there was something he wasn't saying. But it was like he wanted me to ask him what it was."

Pamela didn't know what to say to that. A prickle of fear and guilt pierced her as she thought again about the conversation she'd had with him about Thabo's suicide. The phone in her hand felt like lead. What would Ama think if she told her?

"Are you okay?" Ama asked, when Pam didn't answer, "Pam?"

"Listen, Matlakala is calling me. I'm going to put her through. Matlakala, Pam's on the other line."

"She's gone silent on me, because I said something about Mandla."

Pamela quickly pulled herself together. She didn't want her friends thinking anything was wrong.

"I'm here," she said. By the way, has anyone heard from Beauty?"

"No, I haven't," Matlakala said.

Pamela watched Mandla make his way to their bedroom.

"Ama, have you?" Matlakala asked

"No, but it's not like her, she would have called me by now."

"Well I was thinking maybe you'd called to kiss and make up."

"No, I haven't. But at least I have resisted the temptation to strangle her." Ama laughed.

"You know what, Ama? You can be really insensitive. You know Beauty has feelings too. And it's hard being alone."

Pamela murmured in agreement.

"Yes, well, I suppose I should be grateful that I have a husband," Ama said bitterly.

"Ama, we didn't mean that," Pamela said.

"It is true after all."

"You have to move on sometime, Ama. Try to use this to your advantage."

"Pam, I can't believe you're saying that," Matlakala said.

"Let her finish, Matlakala. Use it to my advantage by doing what?"

"I don't know. There must be something that Lazaro could be useful for," Pamela said.

"Like what?" Ama and Matlakala said simultaneously.

"Pamela! You're not suggesting she use him for his body, are you?" Matlakala said.

"Oh, my God! Is that what you think I should do? Sleep with my husband's brother? I don't believe this."

"Ama, that's not what I said. I only meant … Hey, what was that noise?"

"What? It's not from my side," said Ama. "Matlakala, what was that?"

"It's Joe. Guys I have to go".

"Matlakala, what is he doing? It sounded like he's breaking something?"

"He's trying to open the door. I changed the locks."

"You did what? When?"

"This afternoon. Guys I have to go. I'll talk to you later."

"Okay, but call us as soon as you can."

Matlakala hung up the phone and rushed to the front door. Joe was hollering now, and beating repeatedly against the door.

"Joe, stop that! You'll break my door," she shouted over the noise he was making. The banging stopped.

"Open the door then," his voice came from the other side, calm but threatening.

"No, I can't do that," she said, taking a few steps back. "Why don't you go back to Dineo?" Matlakala squeezed the woman's name out. Since that first shocking phone call at 4 am, the woman had phoned Matlakala several times, becoming cruder and crueller each time. Matlakala heard Joe shifting around. She wondered what he was doing.

"Matlakala, open the door," he said again. His voice was slightly muffled by the door pane, as though he was leaning his face against it.

"What's locking me out going to solve? Let me come in and we'll talk about things."

These were more words than he'd said to her in a very long time. Deep down she did want them to work things out, and talking it through might help some. Slowly, Matlakala walked to the door, unlocked and opened it. Joe came in and closed the door behind him. He looked a bit dishevelled and tired.

"If you wanted to get my attention, there are better ways to get it. Now, I'm listening," he said, leaning against the door. Matlakala looked at him, hesitant. But she had started this, so she might as well finish it.

"Joe, this isn't working. It hasn't been working for a while. Ever since you got retrenched, things have changed," Matlakala said, averting her eyes.

Joe sighed. "Okay, look, could we continue this in the morning? I'm really tired."

"No, you said you were listening, and if we're not going to talk about this tonight you can leave my house."

"Are you threatening to throw me out, Matlakala? Have you forgotten who I am?"

"Yes, and I was hoping you'd care enough to remind me."

"Look, Matlakala, it's late. We can talk tomorrow." Joe started moving towards the bedroom.

"No! Don't take another step." Matlakala, her arms lifted up, placed herself in front of him.

"Get out of my way," he said, shoving her roughly aside. Matlakala's hands flayed in the air, trying to find something to hold onto. An alarmed sound escaped her lips as she fell, her head hitting the hall cabinet, then the tiled floor.

Ama was worried after speaking to her friends. She had tried calling Matlakala a few times, but there had been no answer. Lazaro had come knocking at her bedroom door. Just to check on her, he'd said in his simple way. That bothered Ama. Lazaro's role in her life wasn't supposed to be to care or to worry about her. Ama picked up the phone to call Pamela.

"What is it, Ama?" Things were calm and she didn't want to rouse a sleeping snake in its hole.

"It's Matlakala. I'm really worried about her. I've been trying to call her, but she's not answering."

"Have you tried her home phone?"

"Yes, and it just rings. And Joe's phone is off."

"Well, maybe they're talking things through."

"Maybe, Pam. But I have a bad feeling about this. I think we should go there."

"Ama, I can't go anywhere now."

"Pamela, for God's sake, our friend could be in trouble. You said everything was fine at home."

"You're being paranoid, Ama."

"Call me whatever you like. I don't want to be visited by police officers again. Look, I'm getting Lazaro to take us there, and I'm coming to fetch you now." She put down the phone before Pamela could argue.

When Ama arrived at Pamela's house, her children had eaten their supper and were busy doing their homework. Mandla was still playing with his food. He'd barely looked at her since he'd got home. When Ama asked if he'd mind Pam accompanying her to Matlakala's house, he hadn't shown any emotion. He'd just looked at her, as though to say, do whatever you wish, but know that there will be consequences. Feeling obligated to her friend and tired of her husband's silent treatment, Pamela had left with Ama. But she knew there would be trouble when she got home.

"I don't know why I had to come with you, Ama."

Ama was quiet, regretting her spontaneity. She didn't know why she was doing this. She knew it could cause trouble for Pamela. She was worried about Matlakala, but maybe it was also because she didn't want to be alone. Maybe she would do anything to get out of that new house that reminded her of Thabo. She had to begin her life now and stop clinging to her friends. They have their own lives. She was being selfish.

"Do you want to turn back?" she asked.

"It's a bit late for that. We're halfway there now."

Lazaro glanced questioningly at Ama from the driver's seat. She offered directions as answers. They would check on Matlakala and then go back home.

Pamela was the first to get out of the car, pausing at what sounded like someone weeping uncontrollably.

"What was that?" Ama asked, quickening her steps. She reached the door and started to knock frantically. When there was no answer, she tried the knob.

"Ama, wait. Let her answer the door first," Pamela said, but the door was already open, and she followed Ama inside. Inside the hallway they both stopped, horrified at the sight before them.

"Oh my God. What have you done?" Ama rushed toward Matlakala, who was half lying on the floor, her head held in Joe's arms. Pamela stood rooted to the spot, afraid to move.

"Call an ambulance, Pam," Ama shouted.

"No, no," Joe moaned, his arms tightening around Matlakala as he rocked her from side to side.

"Move, Joe." Ama got down on her knees. "Let me see." She felt for Matlakala's pulse. There was nothing. Matlakala was gone. Pamela stood, frozen, her body losing sensation. She had always thought that one day something like this would happen to her, that Mandla would lose it completely. But she hadn't thought of this: her friends staring down at her, tears in their eyes, especially Matlakala's. She'd cry the most, asking the questions that no one else wanted to ask.

"I'm calling the police," Pamela heard herself say. Ama stared at Pam. Joe stopped his rocking.

"It was an accident," Joe said, holding onto Matlakala.

"It always is," Pamela said staring at Joe. "You can explain yourself to the police." She took out her cellphone. At that moment Lazaro walked through the door. He had been in the car till then, but had grown worried when they had taken long. He took in the scene, walking over to Ama.

"You mustn't touch anything," he said in his quiet way, taking Ama by her arms and pulling her up. Ama weakly allowed herself to lean into him.

"The police will be here in a couple of minutes," Pamela said, eyeing Joe warily. "We have to wait for them to get here, and it could be a while. Let's get some chairs." Lazaro promptly went in search of some.

"Pam? What are we going to do?" Ama said, feeling the loss of human contact next to her.

"I don't know, Ama. The police will be here soon and they'll sort things out."

Lazaro came back with the chairs and the women sat down while he went outside to wait for the police. Joe was still sitting on the floor, Matlakala cradled in his arms. It seemed so bizarre, him holding her like that. The closest Pamela had ever seen them come to touching was Matlakala putting her hand on his shoulder or arm, and that had been a long time ago. And it was always her touching him, never him touching her. How sad, Pamela thought. Now he held onto her as though he could breathe some life into her by squeezing her body to his.

"We came too late," Pamela said after a while.

"We had no way of knowing, Pam."

"I know. It seems like we are always too late."

Chapter 13

"Would you like some coffee?" Lazaro asked when they arrived home. Ama was grateful for the offer. A cup of coffee would buy her time before she had to be alone and face up to what had happened to Matlakala. She still could not comprehend that she was gone. And she could not get the image of her body in Joe's grasp out of her mind.

"Thank you, I'd love some," she said, walking through to her kitchen. It felt strange to be thinking of it as her kitchen. But, after all, it was decorated to her specifications, her dream kitchen, only she'd expected to share it with her husband, not a stranger. Still, she should be grateful for what she had. Ama smoothing her hands over the counter.

"Tragedy has a way of lingering, doesn't it?" Ama asked, watching him.

"I guess so" he said, noncommittally.

"You know, the day before my wedding, something like this almost happened. But that time no one died. There were just a few bruises and a sprained arm. And all that day I couldn't help thinking, how could a woman in her right mind get married after witnessing what a man can do to a woman?" Lazaro stared at her. "But I wasn't given a chance to answer that question …" Tears filled her eyes.

"You should get some rest." Lazaro placed the mug of coffee in front of her on the counter. Then he made for his bedroom. Ama could not help wishing that he had stayed, let her cry, and tried to understand her loss. She had seldom felt more alone, and longed for some reassurance that everything would be alright, even if it was from this strange, cold man.

Pamela had walked into a silent house. She presumed everyone had gone to sleep, and walked straight to her bedroom. Not daring to disturb Mandla by switching on any lights, she found her way in the dark, taking off her clothes. Suddenly, iron-like hands clamped around her neck.

"Mandla?" she gasped.

"For every action there is a reaction," he hissed into her ear. Dragging her over to the bed, his hands tore into the delicate material of her underwear.

"No!" Pamela struggled, but his weight pinned her down. She kept trying to fight him off, her voice rising to a scream. His hand muffled the sound by cruelly clamping on her throat, suffocating her. He grunted as he entered her. Pamela finally gave up resisting as he thrust into her again and again.

Afterwards, she lay motionless and numb, silent tears coursing down her cheeks. She could take many things, him beating her, ignoring her and even hating her, but this was too much.

The next morning, she got up early, and went to fill the bath with hot water. She sat there for a full hour, staring at nothing, hardly feeling the scalding hot water.

Back in the bedroom, Mandla was just waking up. She gave him one glance. Discarding the towel she walked to her dressing table rubbed on some body lotion and applied her make-up. Once she was done, she went to the wardrobe and took out her uniform. Now she faced him.

"Matlakala is dead," Pamela said without feeling. She pulled on her skirt. Mandla looked momentarily shocked, before his expression turned menacing.

"And that's the reason your friend came barging in and dragged you Lord knows where?"

"No, she came because she wanted us to stop it before it happened. But we got there too late." Pamela put on her blazer. "Yes, Mandla. She was killed by her boyfriend, Joe."

For once Mandla seemed at a loss for words.

"Now, I'm going to work," she said. "And by the way, I was thinking of redecorating the house. Add a few coats of paint to the bedrooms and the kitchen, and maybe refurnish the sitting room."

"Your friend just died," Mandla said, "and you are talking about redecorating? Besides, you love that furniture, why would you want to get rid of it?"

"Ama has agreed to use it in her new house, so I won't be losing it," she said. "I want some change, if you don't mind. I'll start tomorrow, since I'm on leave." She checked the contents of her handbag.

"I don't understand this."

Pamela saw his confusion turning to anger.

"I just want something to do, that's all. Something that will keep me, busy, distract me from thinking about Matlakala."

Mandla grunted.

"Fine," he said grudgingly.

Pamela breathed a sigh of relief. He seemed to have bought it. "I'll see you later," she said, and left to catch a taxi to work.

Chapter 14

That afternoon, after work, Pamela made her way to Ama's house. There were many things they had to figure out concerning Matlakala's death, plus she wanted to get some rest before going home. She hadn't slept much the previous night.

Ama showed Pamela to a room where she could sleep for a few hours and told her that Matlakala's family had been contacted and that Matlakala's mother was on her way. At least they would have someone to help with all the arrangements.

After her rest, Pamela went in search of Ama. She was in the kitchen nursing a mug of coffee. Pamela helped herself to some tea and sat down next to Ama. They sat for a while sipping their drinks.

"I haven't slept all night" Ama said.

"Me neither." The saddest thing was that her lack of sleep hadn't been due to the death of her friend. Ama looked at her sideways, and then continued to drink her coffee. "I thought you were going to work," said Pamela.

"I couldn't. Maybe I wasn't ready after all. And now with Matlakala… I guess I'll give it a bit longer."

"Lazaro was a real help last night." Pamela recalled how he had handled the police, and looked after her and Ama.

"I know," Ama said.

"What time did Matlakala's mother say she'd arrive?"

"She didn't say. They want to take her home. This is her home, isn't it Pam?"

"In our hearts she'll always be our sister, no matter where she's buried," Pamela said. She reached out a hand to Ama.

"I don't know if I can go through this again, Pam."

"Oh, Ama, I know. But we don't have a choice. How is Matlakala's mother going to get here? Does she know where we are?"

"Jeffrey is going to wait for her at The Bridge."

"How is he taking it?"

"As well as any of us. The sad thing is that he seemed truly surprised, as if he didn't believe another man could be capable of such a thing."

Ama's words struck a chord in Pamela. Didn't they all make excuses or turn a blind eye? Especially her? What was she going to do about her life? Surely the only answer was to leave her husband. It was clear, as he had demonstrated last night, that if he wanted to, he could easily kill her, and move on with his life. But was it that simple?

"When is Beauty coming back? Do you know?" she asked.

"Her phone is off. Jeffrey tried to get hold of her several times this morning. She should come back."

Pamela chewed. "It's not going to be good when she finds out."

"No." Ama sipped at her now cold coffee.

"Do you know what made her decide to go away?"

"I have no idea. I really hope it wasn't because of what I said to her."

"No, I'm sure that's not it. You know Beauty. Everything's a bit of a mystery with her. You can never be sure why she says or does the things she does." Pamela chewed absentmindedly at her nail. She thought about the redecorations she was planning. The designer would have to remove the furniture before replacing it, putting it in storage. For a moment she fantasised about Mandla coming home to an empty house, with her and the children gone. How would it feel for him to lose everything? Maybe it's what he deserved. Certainly some people would think that.

"She should come back," Pamela said again.

Ama looked at Pamela questioningly. "Pamela, what's wrong?"

Pamela continued to chew at her thumb nail, moving on to her ring finger. One way or the other, Pamela thought, she was going to be free of him, dead or alive. So why suffer in the meantime?

"Pam, what is it? Please, talk to me." Pamela shook her head, unable to speak.

"You have to be strong for me, Pam. I can't face Matlakala's death by myself."

At Ama's words Pamela blinked, as though waking from a dream.

"Don't worry, Ama." She rubbed Ama's arm. "I'm here. Matlakala deserves better than us reduced to basket cases."

"Then what is it that's bothering you?"

"I've finally decided, Ama" Pamela said releasing a sigh. "I'm going to leave him. It's time."

Ama stared at Pamela in disbelief. Then her shock was replaced by fear. "Are you sure?"

Pamela guessed Ama was thinking of Matlakala.

"I haven't figured out how I'm going to do it yet, but I have to start." Pamela's voice was soft but urgent. "Matlakala died because of some useless low life that couldn't see a good thing right in front of him. So, for her, I'm going to treasure my own life and my children's", Pamela breathed deeply, refusing to cry.

"You can come and stay with me," Ama offered.

"No, thanks, but he'd come here and harass you."

"So what are you going to do, Pam?"

"I don't know yet, but I'll figure it out."

"I'll help you."

"Thank you, Ama."

The two women held each other, drawing apart at the sound of a car pulling up outside.

Lazaro came into the kitchen. "Ama, your brother is outside. Matlakala's mother is with him. He thinks it's best you come out to welcome her."

"Thanks." Ama got to her feet.

Pamela wiped at her face and followed Ama to welcome Matlakala's mother.

The woman that waited for them outside was the spitting image of Matlakala, apart from the prominent wrinkles and greying hair. Pamela could have sworn Matlakala had risen from the dead. Ama stepped forward, extending her right hand in greeting.

"I'm Ama," she said, holding the woman's hand tenderly. Pamela followed suit, extending her condolences. The meeting was a sad one. It was impossible not to feel Matlakala's absence, to miss her girlish voice and gentle manners. They all felt it standing there. The group headed inside the house, past Lazaro, who held the door open for them accepting Jeffrey's silent nod with a slight movement of his eyes.

Closing the door, Lazaro ushered everyone into the sitting room. "Would anyone like some coffee? I'll put the kettle on."

"Thank you, Lazaro. We'd appreciate some." Ama turned to Matlakala's mother.

"I would like to take Matlakala's things with me. I'll leave some things of hers with you if you'd like to have them to remember her by. Of course it will take some time to pack. If you ladies don't mind I'd appreciate your help." Matlakala's mother worried her hands. She seemed to be uncomfortable about something.

"Of course we'll help." Pamela and Ama mumbled together.

Matlakala's mother looked around her. She appeared to be searching for the right words.

"Did you know this Joe?" she asked suddenly. Pamela fidgeted in her seat. Yes, they knew him. What was there to say about him? Pamela's eyes drifted to Ama. At that moment Lazaro walked in with the coffee and Ama got up to help him. For a while the atmosphere relaxed, but once the men had finished their coffee and left the women to talk, the tension returned.

Once again Pamela wished Matlakala was there. She'd have known the right thing to say. Pamela released a frustrated sigh.

"Joe was …" she started.

"I'm sorry if it's uncomfortable for you, me asking about Joe," Matlakala's mother interrupted. "It's just that I never got the chance to meet him. Matlakala never got around to introducing him. I just wanted … I don't know. Maybe it's too late for that," she said, trying hard to suppress her tears. But they flowed, and Ama and Pamela joined in.

"You can never really know, can you?" said Matlakala's mother.

"Yes, you can." Pamela was adamant. The other two women were quiet, watching her. "Yes, you do know. It's just a matter of time before something happens, whether good or bad. But all along, you know."

"Pam," Ama said sympathy, in her voice.

"I know, Ama."

"Was she happy with him? I mean truly happy. She never did say anything about their relationship. I just assumed everything was alright, and when she was ready she'd come and introduce him."

"They hadn't been happy for a while," Pamela said. "But we didn't know what was wrong. She never said." Pamela went on to relay the little she knew about Matlakala and Joe's relationship. Matlakala had been her friend, but there was little she could say to the woman weeping in front of her as reassurance. She could not give her any evidence that her daughter had not died in vain.

Jeffrey found Lazaro in the backyard bent over some bottles of diluted paint, a paintbrush in one hand. When Jeffrey came close, Lazaro straightened up and faced him.

"You're an artist," Jeffrey said, not really expecting an answer. Not for the first time, he wondered about this man that he'd allowed to be his sister's keeper, a man she didn't know or love. Well, there was nothing he could do about that now. Ama should plant some grass and flowers back here, he thought, looking around him at the weeds dominating the yard.

"Yes," Lazaro said, turning back to his painting. Although it was unfinished, Jeffrey could see it held the image of person.

"Have you been doing this for long?" he asked, looking closer. Lazaro was silent for a while. Jeffrey knew he was intruding, but being out here was better than being inside, trying to figure out the death and life of another woman.

"I've been painting for as long as I can remember."

Jeffrey looked around for somewhere to sit. "That long?" He made himself comfortable on the ground. The ladies inside the house would no doubt be a while. Lazaro went back to his painting.

"You don't talk much, do you?" he asked.

"No."

Jeffrey persisted. "How are things going?"

"You mean with your sister?" Lazaro asked, turning towards him.

"Yes."

It seemed like Lazaro was not going to answer. But then he put down his brush and said, "I think she'll be okay, with time."

"Yeah," Jeffrey said, feeling the guilt that had been plaguing him for the past few hours, and which he knew would not go away, even with time. Things would have been different if Ama were still living with him. He'd know what was going on in her mind, and wouldn't have to ask a stranger.

"You two seem to be getting along," he said.

"Yes, well we live in the same house, but we don't speak much. We live our own lives. I guess we get along," Lazaro said, going back to his painting. Jeffrey thought he detected disappointment in the man's voice. So, they had lived in that damned house for less than a day and already he was showing his horns.

"Wasn't that what you agreed to?" Jeffrey asked, standing up. Slowly Lazaro turned to look at him. He didn't show any emotion or reveal what was on his mind. Jeffrey became agitated by his silence.

"Lazaro, do you want something from my sister?" Jeffrey said, his voice rising. Lazaro looked at him, unperturbed.

"No."

"Be honest with me, damn it. You're a man, after all. There's no way you can live with a woman in the same house and not want something from her." He knew that he was probably wrong. It was hard to imagine the cool Lazaro feeling passionate about anything. But he couldn't help wanting to direct his frustration at this man, so infuriating in his quietness. There was so much going on in Jeffrey's mind, from worrying about his sister living with this complicated man and Beauty, who was nowhere to be found, God only knew where she was. Thinking about

Beauty, his imagination took him on unwelcomed paths. He feared that one of these days he'd hear that Beauty had been found sprawled in some unknown field, dead, murdered like Matlakala. Feeling suddenly exhausted by it all, he slumped back onto the ground.

"Sorry, Lazaro, it's just that …" He did not really know what he wanted say. For Jeffrey, this was the worst day of his life, and he could tell it wasn't about to get any better.

"What do you want for your sister, Jeffrey?" Lazaro asked.

"I don't know," he said. The future at the moment seemed so bleak. He was tired of telling Ama that everything would be fine, when clearly there was nothing fine about this situation. "If there was some way you could make her happy again … That's maybe one of the reasons why I didn't interfere with your family's decision. I don't know." He paused for a while. "I knew you wouldn't be able to replace your brother, but maybe for a while … I hoped for a while you'd be able to help her grieve, to let go of her loss. And she'd be able to move on with her life."

The two men stared at each other for a while. To Jeffrey's mind, the life that Lazaro led was no life a man would want to lead. What had happened to his dreams, his wishes and wants? As far as Jeffrey could see, there was no way Ama could ever accept Lazaro. Maybe it was better that way. Maybe.

Jeffrey sat watching Lazaro paint. He could see he was creating a beautiful thing. The man could express himself better in colours than in words. Maybe that was it right there; words were far more complicated than colours. Jeffrey sat there watching the world become still in a few simple strokes of a brush.

Chapter 15

A full week had passed since Matlakala had died. Her belongings in her house were packed and waiting to be transported with her mother, who had returned home to take care of the funeral arrangements.

Ama realised that she didn't even know where Matlakala's home was – she knew the name of the place, but not the breeze that blew it, or the clouds that brought it rain. She didn't know where the woman they had known had taken her first steps. It was sad that they'd only get to know her home now when she was gone. She would not be able to show them her favourite spots, or where she'd had her first kiss, or introduce them to her childhood friends.

Matlakala's funeral was to be the following Saturday. Ama hoped that Beauty would have come back before they left on Friday night. She had to be there; Matlakala would have wanted it. Now, packing the last of Matlakala's things with Pamela, Ama looked around the empty house. It was as though she'd never been there, as if Matlakala's mother had come and taken her away. How easily a life could end, she thought.

Ama looked about for anything they might have missed. In the back of her mind she searched for the sweet Matlakala – maybe she'd turn up in one of the rooms, babbling on about something to do with love and how every individual deserved to be loved.

"Let's go, Pamela," she said. She had had enough. The whole week they had toiled, packing things up, hoping to fit the life of a twenty-four-year-old woman in boxes and refuse bags, all because of some useless man who could not appreciate what he had had.

As hard as she tried, Ama had found the last week difficult to handle. Even Lazaro was showing signs of concern, in his way. Though he did not show it like others, she could see that he cared. And that fact, for some reason, didn't bother her as it might have before. She knew it was because she was feeling vulnerable and in need of comfort, even if it had to come from him.

She picked up the last box and followed Pam outside, closing the door behind her and leaving Matlakala's house for the last time.

The news was a shock when it reached her ears. It hadn't even been meant for her ears. On the seat in front of her, Beauty listened to the conversation between two women, talking ceaselessly as commuters do on their way home. The story they were retelling had caused Beauty's heart to miss a beat. The darkness outside the taxi speeding down the Soweto highway thickened, absorbing everything else and leaving her isolated on an island of darkness – it was as though she was in a dome-like space where every sound and every word said was heightened, but she couldn't feel or hear herself. The streetlights did nothing to penetrate the dark and horrific space she was in.

The words pierced her mind: "Matlakala, you know, the one who lives in Pimville, Zone 1. The paper said she was an author or something like that. She was killed by her boyfriend. He found her at home and just killed her."

"Everyone knew he was bad news. I don't even know what she was doing with him."

Beauty felt her stomach churning up the food settled within it, but the commuters went on with their tale. The journey from The Bridge to home was a long one. In the taxi she couldn't cry, scream or let loose all the expletives she wanted to aim at that sorry excuse of a man.

"Short left," Beauty said when the taxi got close to her home. Alighting from the taxi she walked the few paces to her gate, tears clouding her vision. She didn't even notice that the dumping site had been removed. She felt like stopping and letting it all loose. Thank God Joe was behind bars or there would be hell to pay. Beauty let herself into her house. As always it was dark, but today for some reason this disturbed her. There was too much darkness outside; a little light in the house would help to diffuse the clamour in her mind. She switched on the light, and felt a bit better.

"Beauty." Her mother's voice was weary, as though she had been vigilantly waiting for her. Beauty felt a pang of guilt. She had been gone for a full week. Her mother hadn't even known where she had been. For a full week she hadn't been able to communicate with her, because there'd been no reception in the cottage she'd stayed in. She hadn't spoken to anyone, not even Jeffrey. Her heart had broken a little. Even though that was the way she'd wanted it.

"Beauty?" She could hear her mother shuffling around.

"Yes, Ma. I'll be there in a minute." She hurried down the passageway. She felt like a schoolgirl anticipating seeing her mother after a long day at school. Beauty reached her room, switching on lights as she went.

"You're back", her mother said, sitting on Beauty's bed. Her eyes moved curiously over her. Beauty could tell she had so many questions, but had no way of asking. Well, she didn't want to answer anything at that moment, especially after hearing about Matlakala. All she wanted was to get into bed and wait for the morning. And when the sun showed its face, she'd go to visit Joe in prison. It would be the last time he saw any visitors, if she had anything to do with it.

"Yes, I'm back. How have you been?" she asked, putting down her bag and beginning to unpack.

"I've been fine. Just a little lonely, I suppose."

"Well I'm back now," Beauty said. Beauty's eyes scanned her mother's scarred face, seeing it more clearly after a few days apart. Impulsively, Beauty went over to her and took her calloused hands in hers, then wrapped her arms around her.

"Matlakala is dead," she heard herself say. Tears choked her, but she wouldn't let them fall. "I wish I hadn't left. I'm selfish sometimes, Ma."

"You wouldn't have seen it coming, baby. You're not responsible for anyone but yourself. Not even me."

"But if I had been here …" Beauty started to pull away.

"Relax, let me hold you for a while." Her mother held on. "A few days alone can make a person face life, whether or not they want to."

"What do you mean?" Beauty asked, already afraid of what her mother was saying.

"Nothing, it's just that there'll come a time when I'll have to let you go. You can't waste your life away babysitting me."

"Don't say that. I think I've heard enough bad news for one day." Beauty moved away and busied herself taking off her clothes and getting into her nightdress. She would finish unpacking the next day.

"Can we sleep now? I have a tough day tomorrow. Whatever you have in your mind, Ma, forget it. I'm not going anywhere." Beauty waved for her mother to move aside.

"One day that Jeffrey of yours will come wanting to take you away. It's only a mother's job to prepare for such a day."

"Forget about it, Ma." Beauty got under the covers. "That's not going to happen." She didn't want to think about Jeffrey, let alone speak about him. As far as she was concerned, Jeffrey was in her past. Beauty closed her eyes focusing on one man, Joe. And the day she had come across the couple in the park. She felt more certain now than ever that it had been him. God help her if she didn't kill that no good son of a bitch. Yet most probably his mother had nothing to do with his behaviour. No, no woman should be blamed for this. The blame lay fully on his shoulders. Beauty fell asleep thinking of ways he might suffer, seeking some solace at the thought of him locked up with untamed, ruthless gangsters who would do anything for a chance to prove themselves or to get a few bucks in their pocket. The next day she felt less sure of things, entering Sun City prison at visiting hour. A thick glass wall separated her from Joe, and in a way she was glad to have the barrier between them to stop her from doing something she might regret.

Joe looked dishevelled in his orange suit. Beauty could see he'd been crying.

"Are you still awaiting your bail hearing?" Beauty asked.

"Yes." Joe's voice was hoarse, and his hands shook slightly. He had nice hands, with long, elegant fingers. Beauty had never noticed that before.

"Why the orange? Aren't you in a holding cell?"

He wasn't bad looking, in fact. She could see why Matlakala had been blinded by him.

"It doesn't matter. It doesn't look like I'm ever getting out of here," he said.

"You're right." Beauty looked at him straight in the eyes. There was no way she would let him get out.

"It was a mistake, Beauty." He leant forward. "I was trying to get into the house, and I pushed her, and she fell on the cabinet. I didn't even see …"

"I don't want to know!" Beauty raising her hands as if to cover her ears.

"She's gone, Joe. Nothing can change that. We can't turn back the hands of time, can we? I just don't know how you can sleep at night knowing you've killed the sweetest woman in the world? How do you live with yourself?" Beauty could feel rage taking over. "She was on the verge of finishing her second book, did you know that? Of course you didn't. You were too busy doing what made you happy, messing around with other women, to bother about her. Obviously you stopped caring a long time ago. But what bothers me the most is why you never just let her go. Why didn't you leave her? She could have lived her life without you. She could have found someone to love her more than you did. That was all she ever wanted. You should have heard her talk about love. Did she ever tell you her thoughts about it? I doubt if you would have listened. But believe me, it would break your heart, because you'd know you didn't deserve her. Despite everything, she loved you. She loved you with all her heart and nothing else mattered. She …"

"Beauty!" Joe's voice was anguished.

"I understand, Beauty. You do whatever you think is necessary." He got to his feet. "But know this: truly it was a mistake. I might be a lot of things, but I am not a murderer. And I never wanted to hurt Matlakala!"

"You never know what you have until you lose it," Beauty said softly, more to herself than to him.

"Yes." He looked at her for a while. One tear ran down his face. He wiped it away. "Goodbye, Beauty. Please give her my last respects." And he was gone.

Beauty knew she would not visit again. Whatever the courts decided about Joe's fate, Matlakala wasn't coming back, and nothing that happened to him would change that.

Chapter 16

The stark, grey skies of Polokwane, GaMoletlane, seemed to reflect the events going on beneath them. The mourners who were gathered at Matlakala's home seemed to be building up to mass hysteria. Every so often someone would start wailing uncontrollably, to the point where the funeral proceedings would have to be halted until the person was carried away. It was as though they wanted to hold Matlakala back, keep her for a little longer before she was sent to her final resting place.

The three friends also dreaded that final moment of the funeral ceremony. With every prayer that was said, they knew the dreaded conclusion was closer. Matlakala was gone, and they would have to accept that fact, but it was easier said than done. They sang along with every song, joined in the prayers, declared Matlakala to the heavens, but in their hearts they held her back, wishing that by some miracle she would wake up.

Like Lazaro, Ama thought, her eyes going in search of him. She found him sitting next to Jeffrey a few rows behind her. Lazaro from the Bible, who rose from the dead.

His eyes met hers, and she turned around. He had been kind to her, she had to admit. Ama faced the front again, her eyes turning to the coffin in which Matlakala lay.

The preacher was saying his last words: "The journey to the graveyard will be made by foot." Already the mourners were getting to their feet, to make their way there. This was it. The three friends held on to each other and stood watching as men with shovels heaped soil on top of the coffin and Matlakala was laid to rest. It didn't take long, and within seconds she was gone.

After saying their last goodbyes, they made their way back to Matlakala's home with the other mourners. After talking to various family members, getting food and sitting down to eat, Ama was exhausted.

"I think we should make our way back while we still have the strength," she said to Pamela, hoping she'd be the one to take the lead in saying goodbye to Matlakala's family, especially Matlakala's mother. Pamela was about to do that when an old but tough-looking man came to call them into the house. They followed him, Ama searching behind her for Lazaro and Jeffrey. This felt too much like when Thabo had died. Well, at least Pam and Beauty were here. On entering the house they were shown where to sit , while the old man who called them remained standing. He stood there watching everyone. Ama looked at Pamela, wondering what they had missed. Beauty was quiet. The old man finally started to speak. His eyes glinted with emotion, and he drew himself up to his full height, adding a few youthful years to his stature.

"There is no other way of saying this. So I'll get right to it. Today we buried a child of this family, and I hope all of you sitting here are not pretending that that girl died of a disease or that it was her time and we can't do anything but to accept that she's gone. We all know the truth here. She was killed by some boy we don't even know. They had been living together like a married man and woman. And that is what keeps me awake at night. That boy has disgraced this family, and he has taken a child from us. I feel he should be held responsible – he will eventually pay for Matlakala's death once he's sentenced, but this family should hold him responsible too. He should have been the one to bury her, take all the responsibility for her. But since what's done is done, he can now only do one thing. I believe he should marry Matlakala as a way of restoring her honour and this family's honour." He looked around at those gathered, giving his words a chance to sink in. "I've said my piece. Whoever feels they have something to say, this is the time." With that the old man went to find a seat.

Ama sat upright in her chair as the words sunk in. She heard Beauty mumbling something beneath her breath. It seemed she was about to get up and say something when Matlakala's mother stood, wrapping the blanket she was wearing tightly around her. The blanket seemed to weigh her down. But she stood her ground. Her eyes took in the entire room in one sweep.

"Yes, my daughter was killed by a man we didn't know. Yes, she lived with him in her house, and we don't even know for how long. But I believe that's none of our business. That was Matlakala's choice. Whether or not it was a mistake, it was her choice and she lived with it. If she'd wanted us to know about it, we would have known. Now about that man marrying my daughter and restoring her honour and ours: goodness, she's dead! Anything we do from now onwards can't change that fact. And I refuse to ridicule my child this way. I will not sit through a meeting discussing damages and lobola, because she is dead. If a man didn't want my daughter while she was still alive, he has no use of her when she's dead. I hope this is the last time we talk about this. That man will pay for what he did to my daughter and that's where it ends." She sat down. Feeling shaken, Ama was grateful for Pamela's comforting hand on her arm.

Outside, the sun had chased the greyness of the morning away. The yard was deserted, as most people had made their way home. Unable to hold back her fury any longer, Beauty had left the others inside. She wanted to scream. What was wrong with these people? Who said marriage was the destination for every woman dead or alive? Had they forgotten that that bastard was the one who killed her?

Beauty stood there in the open space, feeling as if something was pulling her down, and at the end of the descent she would crash, breaking every last living cell within her body. A lump rose in her throat, but she held back her sobs when she saw Jeffrey approach her. She looked behind her, hoping for a place to flee, but there was nowhere to go. As he came closer, she wrapped her arms around her body. She hadn't spoken to him since she had left, and she didn't know what to say to him now.

"Hey," he said, looking beyond her towards the house. He must be looking for his sister, Beauty thought.

"I think they'll be done any minute now," she said, moving sideways to give him space if he wanted to head towards the house. He didn't move, and this time his eyes came back to her. He didn't say anything, but simply stared at her. Beauty felt awkward and somehow guilty beneath his gaze.

"When do you think we might have that talk?" His manner was cool, revealing nothing.

"Is it still necessary?" Beauty asked. She had accepted the fact that she might end up alone for the rest of her life, and she didn't have the strength to do anything about it.

"You tell me," Jeffrey said still looking at her.

"Jeffrey …" She didn't want to get into this right now.

"Yes?"

Before Beauty could respond, Ama and Pamela walked out of the house. Ama looked questioningly at Beauty.

"Are you ready to leave?" Jeffrey asked, turning to look at his sister "If we leave now we might get home in the early evening."

"Yes, we were thinking the same thing," Ama said, already moving to where they'd parked their cars.

"Where is Lazaro?" Pamela asked.

"He's at the car, waiting," Jeffrey said, watching Beauty walk away from him. Shaking his head, he followed the women to the car and got in with Lazaro.

Ama was driving her own car. For a while the driving lulled her into a state of numbness, the events of the past few months running through her head like a montage. There were her wedding preparations and the colourful cloths sewn together to create a quilt. Her wedding day came next – her white dress shimmering on her skin, the policeman arriving uninvited, and the news of Thabo's death. And then the funeral and Lazaro. Ama sighed deeply. She was no longer sure whether to regret his coming into her life or not. But before she could figure that out, Matlakala's dead form came into view, her unseeing eyes fixed on a spot, and her mouth still open, as though whatever she'd seen had been a surprise. Ama gasped at the image, and, realising that she had suddenly begun to speed, hastily applied her brakes.

"Ama?" Beauty and Pamela said her name together. Behind them Lazaro was slowing down and had put on his hazard lights.

"Pull over, Ama. We have to get out of the road," Beauty said.

"I can't!" Ama screamed the words, her hands shaking in front of her.

"Ama!" Beauty snapped.

"Okay." Ama did as she was told. Lazaro pulled over behind them.

"Can you please tell me what was all that about?" Beauty said, getting out of the car. "We have come from far to bury a friend – must you kill us in the process?"

Lazaro and Jeffrey remained in their car, watching the women.

"Ama, what's wrong?" Pamela asked.

"I wasn't trying to kill anyone," Ama said, still shaking "I was … I saw … you won't understand, Pam. I'm sorry. Maybe you should drive, Beauty."

She opened the passenger door and Beauty got in after her.

"I'm sorry, Ama," she said. "I know you weren't trying to kill us. It's just that everything is so …" She finished with a wave of her hand, lacking the words to explain.

"I know. Things are a little bleak, that's all." Ama smiled at Beauty. "And I'm sorry about the other day. I promised Matlakala I'd apologise once you got back."

"I'm sorry too. I guess Matlakala had more sense than the rest of us." Beauty took Ama's hand in hers.

"She did have sense, but she used it selectively," Pamela said. Beauty laughed. "I guess that's what they call a woman."

"That's not true, because some women live their lives without any fuss or obstacle. Look at you, for instance," Pamela said.

"Bad example, Pam. Even though you might think my life is uncomplicated, believe me it's not. I've got my mother to worry about. I am all she has – there's no one else looking out for us."

"What about Jeffrey?" Ama said.

"No, that boat sailed a long time ago. I don't blame him, though. I guess some women are hard to love."

Ama held her tongue, knowing that her brother wouldn't give up without a fight. But it would be best if Beauty found that out on her own.

"No, Beauty. Women are easy to love. It just hurts when they don't get that love." Pamela said. "Love." Pamela laughed bitterly. "We talk about it as if we know what it is, what it looks like or feels like."

"Matlakala is not here, so no one is going to answer for you there, Pam." Beauty said.

"I'm going to miss her," Ama said.

"Yeah, she deserved better." Pamela sighed. "She deserved so much better."

"Pam, we all do," Beauty said. "You especially."

"I don't know," Pamela said, focusing on the green shrubbery along the highway.

"Pam?" Ama said. "I thought you were going to leave him. And you had a plan and everything?"

"She was?" Beauty said, sounding surprised. "One week away and everything has turned upside down, like some tropical cyclone has been through here."

"Seeing your friend's dead body can do that to you. That, and being raped by your husband." Pamela said the last bit quietly.

"He did what? Pam! When?" Ama looked at Beauty, hoping she hadn't heard Pamela's words and that she was dreaming. "Pam, I can't believe this. What is wrong with that … that …"

"Relax, Ama," Beauty's voice was controlled but angry. "It doesn't matter what he is or when he did what he did. The question is, Pam, what are you going to do about it?" Ama watched Beauty, wondering what was going through her mind.

"I wanted to leave him, you know that, Ama. But before we left to go to Matlakala's home he said something that made me think it wouldn't be wise for me to do anything that would upset him."

"You're thinking about his feelings now, Pam?" Ama said. "What about you? You can't go on like this. You took the first step; you just can't give up now."

"Yes, she can," Beauty said coolly.

"Beauty!" Ama said. "You are not helping."

"Pam has decided. What else can we do?" Beauty said, her voice still detached. Ama was seething. What was wrong with Beauty? She was the first to jump at a woman who allowed herself to be exploited by a man. How could she let this go?

"Beauty, it's not like I …" Pamela began.

"I know," Beauty said, her eyes on the road. Ama felt more tired than ever. She could imagine the conversation that was to follow. The only difference was that for once Beauty was not shouting obscenities or storming off. And for once they were facing the truth, without any of the illusions they usually hid behind.

"If there was another way out of this I would grab it with both hands," Pamela was saying. Her words sounded sincere, as though in truth if there was another way she'd take it. But of course she sounded sincere because she truly believed there was no other way, other than leaving her husband and risking his wrath, which she was not willing to do. So the illusions were still there after all. She wondered what excuse Pamela would come up with next.

"Oh, there is another way," Beauty said. Something in her voice worried Ama. They should just stop talking about this, she thought. Or next week they would be burying Pamela. They'd cry, find a foster family for her children, and then everything would eventually go back to normal. At least Mandla would be in jail, among people who would hit back if he tried anything.

"No, I can't upset him. I never thought he would go as far as to rape me. Now I don't know what he might be capable of," Pamela said, fear apparent in her voice. "And I don't want to find out."

"You won't have to," Beauty said.

"But if I try to leave, I will," Pamela said, her eyes dilating.

"No, you must keep him calm," Beauty said. Ama sat at the edge of the back seat.

"And do what?" Ama said.

Beauty slowed the car down as they came to the next toll gate. She counted the exact amount needed and handed it to the cashier. The bar lifted and they were off again.

"So, are you going to tell us?" Curiosity mixed with fear in Pamela's voice.

"Its simple, Pam, think. What do you *want* to do about it?"

"I don't know, Beauty. Get out before he kills me. Kill him. I don't know." She flung out her arms in despair.

"If I were you, I would kill him and bury him where no one would find him. It's simple Pam: you just poison his food, he dies, and we come and bury him far away."

Ama stared at Beauty.

"No, wait. I never said I wanted to kill him. He's still the father of my children," Pamela said, her hands clutching the sides of her seat.

"Fine, Pam. Well, like I said, it depends on what you want to do about it." Beauty looked up at the rear-view mirror. "I think Lazaro wants to stop. Oh, there is a filling station up ahead, good."

Beauty found a parking space and stopped as Lazaro appeared at the window.

"Are you okay, Ama?" he asked.

"I'm fine," she said, once again noting Lazaro's kindness.

"Would you like anything to drink?" he asked.

"Let me come with you," she said, and together they walked towards the quick-serve shop.

Beauty stared after them. She remembered what she'd said to Joe at the prison. Matlakala was one of those women who was easy to love. She breathed a steadying breath. When you don't want something, you let it go. It should be that simple. Of course that notion would work in an ideal world, where people were not selfish and cruel and didn't spend their lives hurting each other. Unbidden images of her mother's scarred and deformed body came to mind. A long time ago, a man had taken from her and her mother any chance of a normal life. Since then they had lived like monsters, finding comfort in darkened rooms far away from staring eyes. Beauty shivered, watching Ama returning with Lazaro.

Jeffrey stood outside Lazaro's car watching Beauty and wondering yet again why he put himself through this. He could easily find someone else who would appreciate his attention. But there was only one Beauty in this God forsaken world, Jeffrey thought. If only she knew.

Walking up to her side, he was surprised when she didn't move away. He wondered what she'd do if he kissed her right in front of the others. Feeling suddenly reckless, he bent down and gently grazed her lips. Beauty didn't try to resist.

"See, I just can't let go." He smiled at her.

"Yeah, we all have some kind of defect." She looked at him for a while, as though she were seeing him for the first time. "Would you like something from the shop?"

"No."

"Okay, then. I'm going to get something to drink." Jeffrey stared after her. It was as though they were two school kids, learning the ways of romance. It was a start, though, Jeffrey mused.

Back on the road, the three women were quiet, each preoccupied with her own thoughts. Pamela had stayed in the car while the others went to the shop, not sure if she felt steady enough to walk. Now she was going over their earlier conversation in her mind. It was crazy. There had to be another way out. The question Beauty had asked repeated over and over in her thoughts, to the background sound of Ama opening and closing sweet wrappers. Everything was too noisy and confusing.

"Will you stop that?" she said finally.

"What?" Beauty asked, turning to look at her.

"I meant Ama."

"What did I do?" Ama asked.

"Never mind, it doesn't matter." Pamela went back to her thoughts. But the question was still there: "What do you want to do about it?"

Today she had buried her friend, and she had wished with all her might she had been the one lying in the wooden box. Recently, on a rare visit to the city, she'd wanted to throw herself from the tallest building. What was it? The Carlton Centre. To save herself from this. Was that what she wanted to do?

Before, she had wanted to leave him in peace. Pack up her bags, her children and never see him again. That's what she had wanted to do – she'd believed in it enough to tell Ama about it. But it was not that simple.

She thought about the years of terror and horror – blood, pain, broken bones, scars, screams, resentment, hate, fear and silence. And the pain was still there, always present. She could ignore the humiliation, shame and sense of worthlessness, but never the pain. There was always that pain. Even when she'd got used to the beatings, the pain was still there. Then she thought about the last time he had beaten her, how Ama had helped her, and Thabo's death shortly thereafter. She remembered Mandla's hateful words about Thabo's suicide, and for what felt like the hundredth time, wondered if she should tell her friends what he had said.

"I want to cause him so much pain he'll never forget it," Pamela said. Beauty didn't pretend to misunderstand.

"You don't want to kill him," she said, popping a piece of biltong into her mouth.

"No, death would be a gift. He won't feel a thing when he's dead. I want him alive, I want him to feel everything, and I want him to bleed," Pamela said her hands moving in a wringing motion, as though she was imagining them around his neck.

"So it's physical pain you want?" Beauty asked. Ama sat up straighter at this.

"As much as he tortured me, I want him to feel that tenfold."

"Okay," Beauty said. "Will you open this for me, please?" She handed Pamela a bottle of orange juice. Pamela did as she was asked.

"Thanks," Beauty said, taking a swallow. "You do realise we're going to have to do it ourselves."

"Yes," Pamela said, her voice soft but serious.

"We?" Ama asked nervously.

"Yes, we. There's no way you can't do it, Ama. If we're not in this together, that will be our downfall. Everybody's hands must get dirty. That way we'll be afraid for each other and so we'll protect each other. There'll be no pointing fingers. Anyway, we're not going to kill him. So there's nothing to fear."

"You sound so certain!" Ama shuddered.

"I am. Pam, I am serious. Once we start, we can't go back?"

"Yes."

"I mean, even if things get really messy, there's no turning back."

"We're not going to kill him, so why should things get messy?" Pamela asked, panic in her voice.

"You want pain, physical pain at that. How do you think we're going to achieve that?" Beauty's eyes bore into Pamela's.

"Okay, there's no turning back." Pamela's eyes were wide.

"Okay." Beauty turned back to the road.

"Wait a minute," Ama said. "Have you thought about what you're saying? Never mind the consequences of doing something like this, but you're talking about taking down a man who can easily beat a woman like Pamela to a pulp? Sorry Pam, but you know what I'm trying to say. Who are we against someone like Mandla? We've all seen what he's capable of. I just don't think we're being rational right now. We're upset after Matlakala's funeral. But we don't need to lose our minds."

"Oh, there are ways," Beauty said.

"What are you saying, Beauty?" Ama's voice was frustrated.

"I will explain, but not right now. Let's try to relax a bit and enjoy the rest of this journey. We can meet at your house tomorrow, Ama. Then we'll talk, or not. Who knows? Maybe Pam will have had a change of heart. So take this time to think about everything, Pam. Everything you have been through. I want you to see it all. Don't try to block anything out. And then we'll see how you feel."

Beauty put another piece of biltong into her mouth and continued driving, as the sun made its descent, darkening from orange to purple and blood red.

Chapter 17

Sunday had dawned, bright and promising. Pamela had spent most of the night lying awake, thinking. Her decision hadn't been hard after all. When she had arrived the previous night, Mandla hadn't been there to shatter her hard-won resolution. She knew his mere presence might have killed any potential plan of action, replacing it with fear, what-ifs and the thought of years of more of the same dragging by, fear preventing her from doing anything. But now she felt ready to take the first step.

She got up, did some chores and made breakfast for her children, marvelling at their laughter as they sat around the table, chatting and teasing each other. Things were always more relaxed when Mandla was out. They were fine and healthy, she thought. Should she be asking for more than that? Maybe not, but she wanted more for them, much more, and it was time she got it. After breakfast she began preparing the Sunday lunch so they'd have something to eat while she was out plotting to the best of her ability with her friends. Did this make her evil, she asked herself while stirring her stew. Maybe. Maybe she wanted to know what it felt like, to watch her tormentor cowering away, cringing in fear because she had power over him. She wanted to see him on his knees, begging for his life.

She shook her head. Did she really want to turn into him?

"Mom?" Pamela looked up to find Sizwe staring at her.

"What?"

"What's wrong?" he asked. "You look angry."

"It's nothing, Sizwe. I'm not angry, just a bit tired."

"It must be from yesterday, the funeral," Sizwe said. When had he become so grown up? She turned her attention back to her cooking, relieved that he could not read all of her thoughts. If he knew what was really going through her mind he would not be so sympathetic.

Pamela finished up her cooking. This was her way out, right or wrong. It was the only way. If, later, she was judged, so be it. She'd been the good, Christian wife, and it hadn't brought her a piece of heaven yet. Instead, life proved to be hellish, and she was prepared to meet the devil to taste a bit of paradise.

Pamela made her way to Ama's house, hesitating briefly at the gate before straightening her spine.

"I'm doing this for me," she said to herself, and carried on.

At Ama's, Beauty and Ama were waiting in the sitting room, mugs of coffee in front of them. She looked at both of them, a grateful smile gracing her lips.

"Where do we begin?" she asked, sitting down opposite them. Ama turned towards Beauty in anticipation.

"First things first: where is Lazaro? We don't want anyone coming in and surprising us. No one besides us must know about his," Beauty said.

"I'll go and check. But I think he's out back – that's where he spends most of his time." Ama got up to go and find Lazaro. Beauty looked at Pamela from where she sat.

"Are you ready?"

Pamela nodded.

Ama returned a few minutes later, looking flushed. Pamela swallowed nervously.

"The second thing is that we must remain as normal as possible. Ama, don't get so excited, and Pam, you need to hide your nerves. I know it won't be easy, but any change in our behaviour will be noticeable, and we don't want to draw attention to ourselves. Not if we don't want to get caught. So stay cool when you are around other people. We've just buried Matlakala, so it's understandable that we are not quite ourselves. But otherwise try to act the same. Is that clear?"

Both women nodded in agreement. "Now, about the plan. When do you want to do it?" Beauty asked, looking at Pamela.

"I don't know," she said. She hadn't thought that far. All she had thought about was Mandla grovelling at her feet. "Must we choose a specific date?"

"Yes, I think we must. But it can't be too sudden. There has to be something that builds up to it."

"I don't follow," Ama said.

"The point is that it should not seem orchestrated, otherwise we'll find ourselves in jail."

"So what do you propose?" Pamela asked, starting to see the complexity of the whole situation.

"We have to drive him crazy, slowly and publicly, so that everyone sees it and will be able to give testimony to anything that might happen afterwards, when the police start to investigate. We'll drive him crazy to the point where he goes after you, and everyone will think what happened to him was self-defence. So I want you to think, Pam, what would really get to him, enough to make him behave out of character in public?"

Pamela nibbled on her fingernail, deep in thought. If he saw her with another man that would definitely drive him crazy, but he'd kill them both before she achieved her goal.

"She could make sure he sees her with another man," Ama voiced Pamela's thoughts. "Yes, that could work."

"No, the man would deny being involved with you. He'd know you were married, so he'd be careful of being seen with you in public. It has to be something characteristic of you – something that doesn't raise any questions. And even if they are raised, there should be a concrete answer for them."

"I don't know if this will help, but … Ama, do you remember when I told you that I was leaving Mandla, I had mentioned to him that I wanted to redecorate the house? My plan was that I'd take a few things of mine and the kids in the guise of redecorating the house, and leave afterwards. But I didn't have the guts to see it through."

Beauty clapped her hands. "That's it! That's brilliant. You can redecorate your house."

"I don't get it," Ama said. "How will that drive him crazy?"

Beauty got to her feet as the plan formulated in her mind. "Okay. The plan is, Pamela, you're going to call an interior designer to help you with the redecorating. The designer comes to your house and you discuss exactly what you want to change. Do you have somewhere you can take your kids when the time comes?"

"Yes." Pamela had thought about this. "They can go to my brother. He lives in Middleburg."

"Does Mandla know him?"

"Yes, but he hates him," Pamela said with a grimace. The man hated everything she loved.

"Hmmm, that won't do then. When Mandla starts calling around your brother will be the first person he contacts, because there's already some hostility there, and your brother will react if he has something to hide. There has to be someone he doesn't know."

"There's no one," Pamela said, desolation in her voice. "Don't worry, we'll figure something out. There's always a way," Beauty said.

"So what happens next?" Ama asked as she watched Beauty.

"After finding a place to take your kids, the interior designer will remove the furniture in your house. When Mandla comes home he'll find nothing except a letter that you wrote to him. In the letter you're going to tell him that you've left him for another man, taking everything that you own with you. That will definitely drive him crazy. We need people to see him lose the plot. He will go after Pam, and no one will believe him that she attacked him. It will look like self-defence."

"But I'm not the cheating type."

"Yes, but he thinks you are. Why do you think he gave you a curfew?"

"I hadn't thought about that."

"The fact that you just didn't leave, you took everything with you, will make him go mad. And hopefully he'll question people and harass some as he tries to find you. Now comes the hard part. You have to invite him for lunch at a public place under the pretence of wanting to talk. And then you spike his drink with sleeping pills. Ama will have to get those for us. Once he's drowsy, we'll take him to your house. Then we'll tie him up with something non-abrasive but strong, and wait for him to wake up. And then you cause him all the pain you want."

"What if he doesn't react the way we want him to?" Ama asked. "And I still don't see why we have to go to the trouble of hiring an interior designer when we can just remove the furniture ourselves?"

"You must have faith, Ama. Patience and caution are key here. The interior designer makes our plan convincing. Mandla won't suspect anything. Also, we need somewhere to store the furniture, and they can offer us that. Are you going to work tomorrow, Pam?"

"Yes."

"Check your schedule while you're there. We need to do this on a day Mandla thinks you are at work, but you must ask someone else to cover your shift. Remember, act normal. I'll see you ladies." Beauty made her way to the front door. Ama and Pamela stared after her, flabbergasted.

"Are we crazy for allowing her to get us into this?" Ama asked.

"She's not getting us into anything. I'm the one getting you all into this. Beauty is just trying to get me out, and for the life of me I hope she succeeds."

"I don't know about this." Ama stood up and collected the mugs of coffee.

Pamela sensed she was having cold feet, but she wasn't sure why. Ama had seemed enthusiastic before.

"What do you want me to do, Ama?"

"I don't know, Pam. Maybe it's just me. I'm a coward," Ama said. "I want you to get out, but suddenly I'm not sure if this is the right way."

"There's no right way. Whatever we do there are risks, uncertainty. Ama, I thought you would be the one reassuring me. But now it sounds like you are pulling out before we've even begun." Pamela looked at Ama, her eyes showing her hurt. Ama turned towards her, looking stricken.

"Pam, I …"

"You know what, let's leave it for now. We can talk to Beauty again. But now I need to get back before Mandla starts wondering where I am. He must be home by now. I'll let myself out." Giving Ama a quick hug, she left.

A few minutes later Beauty walked into Ama's kitchen. Ama looked at her. She didn't like what she was doing to Pam – pretending that she was not in on the plan with her. But it had to be done, because they wanted her to be sure, and not feel pressurised into it by her friends.

"Did she bite?" she asked, moving to sit at one of the chairs.

"What if she doesn't go through with it? What if she folds? And what if something happens to her? I wouldn't be able to live with myself." Ama was truly concerned. Maybe Beauty was taking this too far.

"It's all the same, Ama. This has to be her decision, anyway. She has to do it because she's had enough, not because we're here offering her a quick solution." Ama wasn't sure whether to believe her.

"Think about it, Ama. It has to come from her or she'll be back in that house with Mandla faster than he can say I'm sorry. If he ever says that. And all this will be for nothing and you and I will have lost a friend in the process. Now I'll get out of your hair. I think Lazaro is headed this way. Hopefully, you'll tell me what's happening with him soon. Shhh … don't even try to say anything. You'll tell me when there's something to tell. Bye Ama."

Ama watched after her, not sure whether she wanted Lazaro to find her standing there. What did she want to do about him? She stood there, but her brain would not produce an answer. They had been living together for – Ama quickly calculated in her mind – what? Two weeks. And yet it felt like she'd known him longer. He seemed to want the best for her, and he worried about her even though that wasn't his responsibility, or maybe it was. Ama winced at the thought. How could she have forgotten? Lazaro was his brother's keeper. So, of course he'd worry about her. Suddenly she felt tired. She could do with some sleep. The things we want from life, Ama thought, leaving the kitchen before Lazaro entered, and going to her bedroom.

Pamela got off the taxi and walked the distance from Dobsonville shopping centre to her home in a very different mood from the one she'd been in on her way to Ama's. She felt like she was walking around in the Sahara, unable to see north or south. Maybe she hadn't thought it through properly. Maybe she'd figured Beauty would take on all the responsibility and she would simply be the doorkeeper who turned the key and let her in, watching as Mandla experienced some of what she'd felt for the past sixteen years. But in her violent imaginings earlier that day she hadn't pictured who'd be performing the actions that would take Mandla down. She hadn't thought Ama, her best friend, would abandon her at this most crucial point.

Pamela reached her home without even realising it. Seeing the pile of painted bricks she called her home, she was taken by surprise. For sixteen years she had gone in and out of its walls without thought. Now, approaching it, it looked unfamiliar. Somehow she could no longer imagine its interior in her mind – the passageways, curtains, chairs, sofas, kitchen units, tiles. It was a pile of bricks that had seen too much of her pain and muffled too many of her cries.

Pamela placed her hand on the gate, pushed it open, put one foot forward, and looked back at the path she had travelled. She knew that whatever happened from this moment on was her own doing. If it made her evil, so be it. She'd repent later. Closing the gate behind her, she walked into the house to find Sizwe serving lunch. She looked at her watch. It was a little past midday. Good thing she had cooked before she left for Ama's. She gave Sizwe a thankful smile as she walked through to her bedroom.

Mandla was there. He was sprawled on the bed as usual, asleep. Pamela wondered what he had been up to the previous night. But for once it didn't bother her. Whatever he had been doing was his business. And he'd soon pay for it, Pamela thought, giving his sleeping form a hostile stare. Indeed, he'd pay for everything. Pamela moved about, banging doors as she went. Mandla opened his eyes.

"It's lunchtime," Pamela said.

"I told Sizwe I didn't want any lunch and nor did I want to be disturbed." Mandla made a point of turning away from her to go back to sleep.

"Sorry, I didn't know that," Pamela said. He grunted something, already drifting off.

"Mandla," Pamela said, apprehension suddenly overwhelming her. Careful, she told herself. Don't act weird. "Mandla?"

"Hmmm!" His growl reverberated through the room and inside Pamela, making her close her eyes as the sound sent fear running down her spine. She steadied herself. This had to be done. Taking a long, slow breath, Pamela plunged in.

"You do remember that I wanted to renovate the house. I was …" Mandla turned over so fast that her words became lodged in her throat.

"Your friend is buried, isn't she?"

Pamela looked at him in confusion. Yes, Matlakala was buried. What did that have to do with anything?

"Well it seems you coped well enough without having to turn the house upside down." Pamela blinked at his words. Of course, she'd said she'd wanted something to do while the funeral preparations were underway.

"Yes. And I still want to …"

"No, I like the house as it is. Can I go to sleep now? Close the door behind you." Mandla plumped up his pillow and lay down again. Pamela stood there staring at him, her heart racing. It wasn't too late to quit, she thought, turning to go to the kitchen.

It had been a long while since she'd opened up shop. Beauty looked at the throng of people waiting for her hands. She had a long night ahead. It seemed some of the women wouldn't go home until their hair was fixed. Beauty's fingers increased their pace as she plaited the hair on the head in front of her. In a few minutes she'd have another customer seated there, and on it would go. This was what she knew, and she felt more at peace than she had in some time.

Her thoughts turned to Jeffrey, and a whimsical smile came to her lips. She recalled their kiss on Saturday. She swallowed hard, not daring to let herself dwell on it. Quickly, she finished with her client. Turning from side to side in the mirror, her client declared to be satisfied with the results. She paid Beauty, and the next customer took her place.

By the time Beauty had finished all the clients, it was just past ten o'clock. Her feet ached and her fingers cramped. Beauty walked into the house, switching on lights as she went. She was getting used to the lights. Ever since the night she'd come back from her holiday and heard about Matlakala's death, it hadn't seemed to matter what she could see any more. She found herself wanting to take it all in, until she no longer really saw, or cared, what was in front of her.

Beauty waited for her mother's usual call, but it didn't come. She must be asleep, she thought. She went to the kitchen to get something to eat. As usual, her mother had cooked their dinner. Beauty served herself, taking her plate with her to her bedroom. She switched on the light in there too. Placing the plate of food on her dressing table, she quickly took off her clothes and made a detour for the bathroom at the end of the passageway. She spent a few minutes having a quick shower, then returned to her room wrapped in a large towel. Without thinking, Beauty let the towel fall while she was standing in front of the full-length mirror. She studied herself, allowing herself to take in everything, from the eyes looking back at her to her shoulders, her breasts and her flat stomach. And there was the scar. It stood out, grotesque and alien from the rest of her body. The scar was there, but she couldn't remember the pain of its creation. The acid had splashed on her side, running down to her thigh, eating away at her clothes to find her skin. She had screamed. Her mother had been screaming too, from where she lay on the floor. No, it had been more of a moan of pain and supplication emanating from her mother's lips. Beauty hadn't felt her pain as she had flung her small body across her mother's, trying to protect her.

Beauty turned around, showing her back to the mirror. There were no scars there. Her mother had soaked up the acid before any could reach her skin as she lay across her, staring up at her father. Beauty blinked and turned around to examine her scar again. The 13th of May 1999: it didn't seem so long ago. Beauty stood, absorbed by her scarred tissue, as the events of that day played out in her mind. At that moment her mother walked into the room. She sent Beauty a look and went to sit on the bed. Beauty reached for her nightdress and put it on.

"Don't stop on my account," she said. Beauty picked up her food and sat down. Her mother watched her eat.

"Do you want to tell me what you saw when you were looking at yourself in the mirror?"

"It's nothing I haven't seen before, Ma."

"Beauty, I don't think you want to see. You'll never let yourself see, will you?"

Beauty kept her gaze trained forward. The food she was eating lost its taste. She couldn't eat any more, and nor could she sit here and listen to her mother speaking in riddles.

"I'm not getting any younger, Beauty. One day you'll have to face this ghostly house by yourself. And ..."

"Maybe that won't be such a bad thing. It's my home, after all," Beauty said standing up abruptly, her plate in one hand.

"Is it your home, Beauty? You're hardly ever here, except to sleep."

"I have a salon to run. I can't sit around and starve." Beauty's voice rose slightly. "What's gotten into you tonight? I've had a long day. Why must you burden me with ... with ...?"

"With what?" her mother asked, her hurt showing in the scarred and disfigured face.

"Ma, please."

"You're switching on the lights for the first time in a very long time. And for once I was glad to see you looking at yourself, inspecting your body in a way you haven't done in a long time – maybe you haven't really looked at yourself, ever. You were only a child, baby. Fourteen years old. Maybe, I don't know, maybe I was hoping; when I saw you looking at yourself in the mirror, that you are ready to let it all go, to see the here and now. If you could look past me, maybe you'd see yourself living, feeling, tasting, crying, loving, and maybe you'd include that boy Jeffrey in all of that." She ended her speech with a tender smile.

"You were hoping for too much, then," Beauty said, slowly walking out of her room with the plate.

"Beauty," her mother called after her. But for the first time she did not answer the sing-song call and her mother did not shuffle after her. Beauty's heart ached. She could no longer hold back the thoughts and feelings she had been trying to block for years, and she wept. After what her father had done, she had learnt to live with her horrific memories, locking them away in a part of her mind she seldom accessed. Yes, she had been young, but she had survived. She had averted her eyes from her scars. And she had lived through her father's hatred and rejection. She had become strong and independent, looking out for herself and her mother. She had kissed men and entered into relationships, but the minute anything got too serious, she would back out, rather than having to face any horrible explanations. The leaving had been easy: black men don't stick around when a woman isn't putting out. So at least she had known another human being's touch, and she had been content with that and no more. But she would never allow anyone to see all of her – to see the horror she and her mother were hiding. She had held the world at arm's length, moving swiftly within it, rejecting anyone who could see too much, except for Jeffrey. He had lingered like a vine, and her mother wanted her to let herself be entangled by him. Her mother called it living, loving and feeling. It was the feeling Beauty was afraid of, because in the end she knew she would have to let herself feel everything, all the sadness and pain, if she allowed Jeffrey to see too far. Many years ago her father had seen inside her, and he hadn't liked what he saw, so he had chosen to burn it all away.

Beauty neatly covered her food, saving the leftovers for tomorrow. Tomorrow, maybe her mother would be herself again. She was talking as though she was about to die and leave her alone. Beauty suppressed the thought. She believed her mother still had a good few years left. Now she would wish her goodnight and tell her they could talk again in the morning.

But her mother had returned to her own room. Beauty contemplated following her there, but decided against it – she was bone tired and she didn't want to think about the past any more. Closing her eyes, she remembered what her mother had said about letting go. They said that letting go was a decision. Maybe she could do it. She might not be able to forgive or forget, but maybe she could choose to let go of the hold the past had over her. As for the future, she would have to take each day as it came. With that thought, she drifted off.

She had hardly been asleep a few minutes when her cellphone rang. She reached out for it, cursing whoever was calling so late, her thumb moving to the red button to switch it off. But then she saw the name displayed on the screen. Beauty groaned inwardly. "Hello, Jeffrey."

"Are you awake?" he asked, a hint of amusement in his voice.

"Barely."

"Do you think you can wake up? I'm outside your house."

"What?" Beauty said sitting up hastily.

"I'm outside," he said again.

"I heard you. What are you doing, Jeffrey?" What was going on? Why were all these things happening at once? This was throwing her off course and she didn't like it. People couldn't just come and bulldoze her into doing whatever they wanted, including her mother.

"I came to see you. It seems this is the only way I can get to you."

"Jeffrey, go home."

"No," he said, becoming silent for a while, and Beauty wondered if he had relented. "I could start knocking on your door."

"I'll call the police."

"Fine, then you'd have to come out and explain who I am." Now he was openly laughing. "Please, Beauty. Come outside. I'm waiting in my car."

"I'm coming, I'm coming," Beauty said, already searching for her gown. She tiptoed along the passageway, passing her mother's bedroom. This was crazy, Beauty thought, but an unexpected thrill ran through her. She reached the front door, unlocked it, stepped outside and locked it behind her. The path to the gate was partially illuminated by a streetlight. The cold air of the early hours chilled her face and her slipper-clad feet, reminding her of the inappropriateness of the situation.

On seeing her, Jeffrey had switched on his headlights. He unlocked the door for her. "Couldn't you have visited in the morning?" Beauty said.

"I believe it is morning."

"That's not funny."

"Yes, it is. You need to laugh more, Beauty," he said, lifting his hand to touch her lightly on the cheek. After the briefest contact, he moved his hand away before she could recoil from his touch, as she was prone to do.

"What are you doing here?" Beauty asked, not sure of the situation at hand. Dealing with Jeffrey from some distance was easy. Even discussions about where their relationship was going were easier, because she could be on the defence, using her sharp tongue to get her way. But now he seemed to be asking nothing from her but her presence. Beauty didn't know how to fight with that. And the confined space of the car made it worse.

"I was lonely at the house," Jeffrey said. Beauty could tell he was being serious now, the joking tone gone from his voice.

"You could have gone to see one of your friends," Beauty said, turning towards the house. Hopefully her mother was still asleep. Any mention of Jeffrey would give her ideas, worse than the ones she had already.

"That wouldn't have helped," Jeffrey said, fiddling with his seat.

"Why?" Beauty asked.

"You want an honest answer?"

Beauty nodded.

"Come." He extended his hands towards her. "Answer me first."

"Must everything always be on your terms?"

"Not everything, only the things I can control. And right now I don't feel in control."

"And that scares you," Jeffrey said.

Beauty studied his face in the semi-darkness. His words touched a nerve within her and she felt the familiar desire to move away rather than feel the fear and the loss that had been part of her life for such a long time.

"What scares you so much?" Jeffrey asked. "Is it me, Beauty?"

"No, you don't scare me," she said, her clenched palms opening slightly. Jeffrey was so close that she could feel his breath on her hair. "So were you just lonely?" she asked him.

"To tell you the truth, I was lonely, longing for you."

"Why?" Beauty asked. She knew she sounded like a stupid school girl, but she wanted him to say it.

"Why was I longing for you?" he asked, the words making her realise how ridiculous her question was. But he seemed to be considering his answer.

"Honestly, I don't know. We definitely don't have the most ideal relationship. I don't even know if I can even call it that." Beauty tensed at this, and tried to move away from him again, but Jeffrey held fast onto her. "It's time we were honest with each other."

"And then what?"

"I don't know."

"Maybe it is over."

"Is that what you want, Beauty, truthfully?" His voice was gentle. She wanted him. But she didn't know if she could put into words what she wanted, when she was afraid to reach out and touch it.

"Why didn't you take whatever it was you wanted? It could have made things easier. And maybe we wouldn't have to have this conversation," she said, her hand moving to cover her eyes. Jeffrey became silent for a long time and she thought he wasn't going to answer. With her eyes hidden behind her hand she couldn't see his face. Maybe she didn't want to see, because she had just voiced her innermost thought. Many times she had thought about it. What if he did force her? Take what he wanted. Would it have strengthened their relationship? If ever he had forced her, what would she have done? She didn't know. Jeffrey removed her hand from her face. He seemed to be struggling to compose an answer. "You thought I would do something like that to you?"

"Wouldn't it have made it easier?" She suddenly felt claustrophobic. She wanted to go back in the house and forget this uncomfortable conversation had ever happened.

"Made what easier? Don't you think that you would have resented me, or more likely hated me for doing that to you? I would have hated myself!"

"Then, what is it you want from me?"

"I've asked myself that question many times."

"And?" Beauty held her breath, not daring to look at him.

"I thought coming here and seeing you would give me an answer," Jeffrey sighed.

"And has it?" Beauty asked, knowing the inevitable had come. She clasped her hands in her lap. It was sad: she could easily put any man in his place, orchestrate Pamela's husband's payback, but she couldn't face this man. She couldn't tell him what she wanted with all her heart, without fearing the pain the confession would bring. Now, sitting here in his car, she was hurting either way. Better hurt now than later, Beauty told herself, while she waited for him to answer her question.

"I find myself in a very difficult position. I love you, Beauty. I don't know why, I just do. But I can't do this thing by myself. I can't take your rejection any longer. I'm only human, after all. This has to come from you. If ever there is to be anything between us, it has to come from you, Beauty. I just hope you'll find whatever it is you're looking for, because honestly I can't promise I can wait for much longer." He touched her cheek tenderly.

Impulsively Beauty reached out and held him to her. She was desperate to say anything to make him stay, because she wanted him to stay, but she couldn't utter a word.

There was so much to be said that the words choked her. So she just held on, closing her eyes as her body melded with his. At least for that moment she was his. He felt warm, safe and dangerous at the same time. Dangerous because he could see deep within her, through her fears and her shortcomings. He pushed her to see that the life she led was not enough. He made her want to let loose and live, without fear, pain and shame. He forced her to let go of her past, to open it for all to see. The most shocking thing of all was that he'd said he loved her. She still didn't know what to do with that information.

"Come, let me take you back inside," he said, removing her arms from around his neck.

At the front door, he paused. "All I want is for you to trust me enough to be with me, without reservation. To love you and have you love me back." He bent down to kiss her forehead. "Goodbye, Beauty."

Beauty slowly locked up. The darkness around her did not calm her. She couldn't believe she had lived in it for so long. She passed her mother's bedroom door. Suddenly she had a yearning to see her.

"Ma," her voice sounded – loud in the hushed space.

"What is it?" her mother asked. "What are you doing in here?" Her mother's voice quivered with fear, and Beauty followed her glance to a spot on the floor close to the wall, a place she hadn't seen in fourteen years. She felt her skin crawl.

"Beauty, come here!"

Beauty hadn't been thinking when she entered her mother's room. She hadn't thought about the fact that she had not entered that room in fourteen years. The room where her mother had been burnt alive.

"Beauty!"

Beauty promptly moved to the bed and reached for her mother, holding her tight.

"What made you come in here?"

"I had to see you." Beauty's hand went up touch her mother's face. The smoothness of the scars slipped beneath her fingers.

"You know you weren't supposed to have been here when your father came home that day. I tried to send you away, but it was too late."

"I wouldn't have left you alone with him."

"I know."

"And you would have died."

"True, but at the end of it all I would have had a normal daughter who embraces everything in life, a daughter who's not afraid of love." At these words, tears pierced Beauty's eyes. It was true. She was afraid. She was so afraid that she had lost Jeffrey in the process.

"It's over between Jeffrey and I. He was here a few minutes ago."

"Did he say why?"

"Yes."

"Don't you think it's time you told him why you are the way you are? Maybe he'd understand. It all starts with you, Beauty."

"What if he doesn't like what he sees?" Beauty asked closing her eyes.

"Then you'll know he doesn't love you."

"What if he doesn't like you?" A lot of people could not bear the sight of her, to the point that they'd rather ignore her existence.

"This is not about me, baby. I've lived my life. It's time you lived your own."

"Why do you like Jeffrey so much?"

"I've never met him, but I have a feeling that he suits you. He's good for you."

"He suits me …"

"No man would have stuck around with you for so long," her mother said, chuckling softly.

Beauty joined her, a spark of happiness forming in her and, ever so delicately, around them. There was still hope where Jeffrey and she were concerned. He'd said he loved her. Maybe if she trusted his words, she could open her own heart. Beauty held onto that thought as she fell asleep next to her mother.

Chapter 18

Ama had everything laid out on her bed. It had been two months since she'd last worn her uniform. Had it been that long? Yes, in fact it felt longer. She had buried Thabo, settled in with Lazaro, buried Matlakala, and now she was conspiring to punish Pamela's husband. And she hadn't spoken to Pam for two weeks, ever since she'd left her home thinking she had betrayed her.

It was time to go back to work. People died, and life went on. She hadn't spoken to Matron about returning: she figured if she just showed up nobody would shun an extra pair of hands.

She hadn't spoken to Lazaro about returning to work. Well, she figured there was no reason to say anything. Days went by with few words being exchanged. Their lives remained the same. Separate. He went about with paint-stained hands, a few words of greeting and concern, nothing more. It could have been worse, but Ama longed for some warmth and companionship, not a housemate. Not that she wanted Lazaro. No. He was just a sore reminder of what she had to live without. And she couldn't very well start dating.

Ama cursed, reaching for her uniform. Her mind turned to Pamela again. They had to let her make the decision on her own. Ama just hoped she wouldn't take too long. The waiting was getting to her.

She buttoned her uniform. She grabbed her cellphone as she made her way to the kitchen. Lazaro was there. Even though he rarely said anything, his presence was felt. Ama looked at his blank face: she could see the resemblance between him and Thabo. And that fact wasn't helping her one bit. She stood and stared at him. Lazaro looked up.

"You're going to work," Lazaro said. Ama didn't respond. "Is something wrong?"

"Why do you ask?" She reached for the kettle.

"You seem preoccupied," he said, resuming what he was doing. He had a funny way of coming out from wherever it was he spent his time in his mind at random moments with some observation, and then suddenly shutting her out again. It bugged her.

"If there was something wrong, would you even care?" Ama said, the resentment she felt barely concealed in her voice. She knew she was being irrational. What did she expect from him? "That's what I thought, Lazaro. I'm going to work," she said. As she reached the front door her cellphone rang.

"Ama …" Pamela sounded worn out.

"Pam?" Ama tried to remember what Beauty had said she should do if Pamela called. Don't pressurise her. It has to come from her. It has to be her idea.

"It took me a while to come to terms with the implications of what I have to tell you," Pamela said. But I have to tell you this before I take it to my grave."

"Pam." Ama felt fear choke her. "What's happened? Did Mandla hurt you? Must I come over?"

"No. Ama, listen to me. It's about Thabo."

Ama felt her body freeze over. She stood there, paralysed. What about Thabo? Thabo was dead. What more was there to be said about him?

"Okay, I'm sorry to bring this up, but you have to know." Pamela cleared her voice, "Thabo might not have committed suicide. Mandla …"

"What?" Pamela couldn't be saying what she was saying. She must have screamed the word, because she noticed Lazaro had come to stand at the kitchen door, watching her.

"Mandla might have been involved somehow, Ama. I don't know how, but I think he had something to do with his death."

"Why are you telling me this?" Ama's voice surprised her with its steadiness.

"Because, Ama, what I'm about to do might kill me. I didn't want to take this to my grave."

Ama felt suddenly weak. She had to sit.

"Look, Pam, I have to go now …"

"Ama, please don't hate me for this. At the time I didn't know what to do, and you were going through a lot. Thabo was about to be buried and that thing with Lazaro was driving you crazy. I didn't know what to do, Ama."

Ama's eyes went to Lazaro. He looked worried.

"I've got to go, Pam," she said, ending the call. Her brain hummed. Just when she'd thought things were returning to normal. She was tired of feeling sorry for herself. She was tired of wondering what tomorrow would bring. She was tired of wanting a perfect life. In her room, she rummaged through her wardrobe. She had to find it, and then she'd know. As she searched, growing frantic, she tossed clothes onto the floor. She was so wrapped up in her search that she didn't notice Lazaro had silently followed her into the bedroom.

When she had moved here she had buried Thabo's suicide note under a pile of clothes where she wouldn't have to see it, and be reminded of her loss. But that had not helped; Lazaro was reminder enough, as was her life in this house, where she slept in the master bedroom, on a queen-size bed, all alone.

At last she found the letter. The envelope was open, but she had never taken out the letter the night she'd opened it. Her fingers carefully unfolded the single sheet of white paper. The handwriting she recognised easily, although the few words scribbled there were not what she'd expected. There was no declaration of undying love nor any explanation of why he had decided to kill himself. It read, simply: "Goodbye, Ama. Things will be better from here on."

Ama looked at it in disbelief. Lazaro came closer, and knelt beside her. He took the note from her, scanned it briefly, and then turned her way.

"It doesn't say much, does it?"

"He wouldn't have to," she said, getting to her feet. Anger rose within her. Pamela's confession came to mind. Maybe there was some truth there.

Maybe Mandla had done something to Thabo, Ama thought, unwilling to acknowledge the fact that Thabo might not have loved her. She had carried that note for a long time, unconsciously hoping that when she was ready to read it, it would ease her pain, that there would be love in his words and an explanation that would justify his actions. Mandla must have done something, she decided, and for that he would pay.

"Ama, I have to tell you something," Lazaro said, getting to his feet. His dispassionate voice grated on Ama's nerves. Another uncaring man, she thought, glancing at him.

"I'm going to work, Lazaro, and I'm already late. If you don't mind." Ama left Lazaro holding the note.

Over the past week Beauty had made a few changes in her salon. She had hired an assistant so that she could spend some time during the day with her mother. She had begun to leave some doors open at home, and a few times, with Beauty's cajoling, her mother had come to sit just outside the front door to see the world and let it see her in the process. From the many glances sent her way by Beauty's customers and employees, she could see some of them hadn't forgotten, while others were too young to remember, but the shock on their faces was the same. They seemed unable to breathe, swallow or look away. Beauty's mother let them have their fill before a cracking laugh pierced the air, and they would quickly turn away.

Another small thing Beauty had done was to start thinking about Jeffrey. At any moment she could call him up in her mind and see him vividly, feel the emotions he conjured up within her. And she accepted them, acknowledged them as reality and nothing to be ashamed or afraid of. All that was left for her to do was to call him. She hadn't figured out what she'd say. She wasn't even sure whether he and she could have a future. She just wanted to open herself up to another human being, and she felt it would be safer if it was Jeffrey. He already knew almost everything. And he'd said he loved her.

Now, Beauty stood in the kitchen arguing with herself about whether to call while she watched her mother outside, laughing away at the world.

Beauty stared at the phone, willing herself to call. She didn't have much to lose. But she couldn't do it. She placed the phone on the kitchen table. She would keep her mind busy with hair. But before she reached the door the phone rang. She snatched it up, hoping it was Jeffrey. But it was Ama.

"Are you ready to do this, Beauty?" Ama's voice was strained.

"What do we need to do to finish what we've started?" Ama stressed every syllable. This would not do. It wouldn't help if they were overly emotional.

"Beauty, what do we need to do?"

"We need something that will make him sleep," Beauty said.

"Valium," Ama declared.

"Valium?

"Yes," Ama said.

Beauty could hear her impatience. Well, it was time to get moving. They had stalled long enough. Ending the call with Ama, Beauty phoned Pamela.

"Pam, are we still on?"

"It was never off, but I thought Ama ..."

"Never mind that, are we moving forward?"

"Yes, but Mandla refused my suggestion of renovating the house. He said I'd ruin it."

"It doesn't matter what he said. Now listen ..."

Pamela had listened as Beauty listed everything she needed to do, and wished she had written everything down. Find an interior designer, make an appointment for Saturday. When Pamela had retorted that she didn't know where to find one, Beauty had fired back: "The internet, Pam."

Now staring at the schedule in her boss's office, Pamela didn't know what she'd tell Mandla about the interior designer. He had flatly refused to allow any renovation of the house. Maybe she wouldn't have to explain. She jotted down the dates from her schedule, up to the third week of the month. Beauty had requested that as well. Everything was happening so fast. Her heart boomed in her chest, and sweat made her clothes cling to her skin.

She felt changed, alive, and nervous too. After a simple call, what she had thought might never happen, what with Ama's doubt and Mandla's adamant refusal was suddenly in motion. It wouldn't be simple or easy. It would take time and a lot of strength. Pamela reached for the keyboard and began to search the net.

Chapter 19

The weeks that followed moved along at a speed that was both dizzying and alarming.

It started on Saturday at midday, when Pamela's appointed interior designer arrived in a flurry of hurried movements, darting eyes accompanied by a quick altering speech. With a constrained smile, Pamela ushered him in to the sitting room, where Mandla had monopolised the television for his afternoon sports. The children had gone to see a movie. Mandla's hostility showed straight away. He moved his eyes from his wife to the man in front of him, not getting up from his chair or offering any greeting.

Pamela tried to remain calm. But to her surprise the interior designer took Mandla's rudeness in his stride. He gave Mandla an assessing glance and settled himself opposite her husband, making himself at home.

"I'm Sipho." He reached out to shake Mandla's reluctant hand.

Despite her nerves, Pamela couldn't help feeling amused.

"I was thinking of redecorating this entire room, making it more lively." Pamela spread her arms to encompass the room.

"I can see what you mean," Sipho said enthusiastically getting to his feet. He inclined his head to the side, one arm held across his chest the other bent at the elbow.

"And I was thinking we need new sofas."

"I can see you want to make a big change. That's good, very good." Sipho shifted his weight onto one leg. "But what about this space?" He walked across to the dining room, which was separated by a pillar. "And this thing?" He pointed to the pillar. "Why don't we use it to create a fireplace for both rooms?"

Before Pamela could answer there was a growl from Mandla, who had moved behind her. She felt his right hand coming to rest on her back. His fingers grabbed a fist full of flesh. Plump as she was, the fist was generously filled. Mandla tightened his fingers, sending a warning. Pamela stiffened as the familiar fear and pain fizzed through her body. Mandla leant closer, his mouth close to her ear.

"We've talked about this, Pam." His fingers pinched her flesh.

"Yes, I know, but now I'll have a professional to help me, so I won't mess up the house like you said," Pamela said as sweetly as she could. She couldn't mess this up now. Mandla narrowed his eyes.

"It's a good idea, you know," Sipho said, seeming impervious to the tension. "Soweto is cold, and a little bit of heat won't kill you. So, what else, dear?"

"Well, the bedrooms also need some work." Pamela pointed in their direction, gesturing for Sipho to go ahead. Mandla's fingers tightened ruthlessly.

"You are going to regret this," Mandla whispered in her ear. It took all she had not to wince at the pain.

"I'll show you where they are." Pamela manoeuvred herself out of his grip. She was grateful to escape, but she knew it would not be for long.

Plastering a smile on her lips, she proceeded to show Sipho the rest of the house. By the time they were done, an hour had elapsed and half of the house had been included in the redecorating plans. Throughout the tour, Pamela registered Mandla's mounting anger, and her anxiety built with every minute. If his pacing and grunting were any indication, her husband was close to boiling point. But she could tell he was biding his time before reacting, waiting for Sipho to leave.

Seizing an opportunity while Sipho had Mandla cornered, Pamela escaped to the bathroom to make a call. Pamela felt her chest tightening as she waited for Beauty to answer her phone. In a few seconds she'd be faced by a very angry Mandla. And this time Pamela could tell he wouldn't hold back any punches.

"Hello." Finally Beauty's voice came through.

"What must I do now? Mandla is furious that I went ahead without his permission." Pamela moved to the bathroom door to listen out for him. She should have thought about this before – what would she do if he came at her, fists blazing? Pamela didn't think she could handle another beating. Matlakala's still body in Joe's arms swam before her eyes. He'd surely kill her this time, Pamela thought.

"Do you think you can pack an overnight bag?" Beauty asked after a minute of silence.

"How am I supposed to pass through the front door with that?"

"Make a plan, Pam, its important."

"If I die, Beauty, it'll be because of you."

"We all die some time, Pam. Pack the bag. You have to do it. Now get out of that house and make your way to Ama's. I'll meet you there."

"Okay." Pamela tried to control her fear. It was near debilitating. She breathed hard to keep it at bay, even though she could feel her skin heating up, her heart crashing in her chest. She was used to it. But somehow what she felt now was different. The fear churned in her stomach, draining her strength. Freedom. She tasted the word, at once sweet and bitter. She had to make a plan. If she was to get out of the house she had to get out with Sipho.

Pamela moved as quickly as she could. She went through her wardrobe, taking out what she needed. Pamela had a feeling she wouldn't be coming back to the house any time soon. Still, she chose clothes that she hadn't worn in a very long time, as though unconsciously she didn't want Mandla to see that her clothes were missing. She quickly went to the kitchen to get a refuse bag. Sipho was there, jotting down notes and making measurements. She gave him a weak smile, and then dashed back to the bedroom. Her eyes wandered to the sitting room where Mandla was sitting watching the soccer match he'd been waiting for. His expression was contemplative, impassive. Pamela knew this was bad. It meant that he was thinking about what he was going to do to deal with whatever it was that had offended him. Pamela shoved her clothes, shoes and uniform into a rubbish bag. Her toiletries she decided to stash on her person. She made sure she had her cellphone. She'd have to call Sizwe later. She took out some money and shoved it into her bra along with her phone. The schedule, she mustn't forget that.

That was it. She looked around to make sure she had everything, and that the room still looked normal. Picking up her refuse bag she went back to the kitchen where Sipho was getting ready to leave.

"I think I'm done for now. I tell you, dear, once I'm done this house will look brand new."

"Yes, that's what I'm hoping for." By the look Sipho gave her, Pamela could tell that her smile was overly bright. "Do you guys do landscaping?" She moved to the back door of the kitchen. Pamela hoped he'd follow without question, "Mandla, I'm going to show Sipho the garden quickly and then I'll show him out." A grunt sound came from the sitting room. Yes, he was still in plotting mode, Pamela thought, and when he came out of it there'd be hell to pay. That made her move quickly. Sipho followed. He didn't even bother to tell Pamela that they did not do landscaping. He could tell something was happening. Pamela held on to the refuse bag, glad that things were going well for now. Sweat was pouring over her – she could smell it. She had to reach the gate first and not make any noise. Avoiding the large window of the sitting room, Pamela held the bag low, trying to keep close to Sipho's side, away from Mandla's view.

She held onto her bag, making inane conversation with Sipho about furniture, paint and fireplaces that could easily be fitted in along a pillar that had held her house, her home, together better than she had. That pillar was right in the middle of her house, holding up the roof and supporting the walls that created her home, but now it was … Pamela didn't want to think about it. Hopefully later, when everything was said and done, and Mandla had been beaten and tortured a thousand times, she'd think about creating a fireplace with that pillar, so that it would not only hold up, but also heat her house.

Sipho said his goodbye, promising to keep in touch, and drove off. Pamela kept walking, clutching her bag as if it were a shield. She had to get away from the house as quickly as possible. Mandla could be waiting. Her children came to mind. She'd made sure they weren't at the house when the interior designer came. She hadn't prepared very well for this, but when it came to her children she couldn't take any chances. Mandla was as unpredictable as a wounded snake. Pamela wondered what would happen when they got home. She'd call Sizwe to make sure they were alright, Pamela thought, patting the phone in her bra.

Pamela decided to make her journey on foot as far as Mmesi Park. Hopefully Mandla would think she was just going to the shops. She'd catch a taxi on Braamfisher Road. It was a long walk. A long walk to freedom, she smiled wryly to herself. Her arms ached, carrying the bag, but it was a welcome pain.

When Pamela reached Ama's house, the sun was beginning to dip. Soon it would be dark.

Ama and Beauty were in the sitting room, as usual hunched over large mugs of coffee. Pamela fell onto a sofa, sighing, with the refuse bag still tightly in her grip.

"I'll make you something to eat," Ama said. Pamela could see she felt uncomfortable. Back in the sitting room, Beauty stared at Pamela.

"Tell me you have your cellphone with you," Beauty said, her voice stern. Pamela tiredly patted her breast.

"Good. From this moment on, when Mandla calls you, tell him that you'll be home soon. Don't say anything specific – just tell him that and then leave him hanging." Pamela looked at Beauty. "Pam?"

"Yes, I heard you."

"This is only the beginning. If you're tired now … I don't know."

"I'm fine, Beauty."

"Fine. Just make sure you're alert all the time. This might turn nasty. You need to be vigilant. We don't know what your husband will do next. Okay, enough about that. Tell me what happened with the interior designer. Did he cause trouble?"

"Yes. He was gay, I think. And you know how black men are around homosexuals. Mandla was furious."

"That's good," Beauty said nodding her head. "The angrier he gets, the better. He'll be irrational by the time we're done with him."

"So, where to from here?" Pamela asked.

"We'll have to move you. You can't stay here. This will be the first place Mandla will start looking."

"What makes you think he'll look for me? What if my being gone works for him just fine? He could find another woman." She knew as she spoke that this was not true.

"I pity whoever he finds, and so should you." Beauty looked at Pamela awkwardly for a while, as though she was assessing her. But instead of disgust, Beauty's face transformed into compassion and an unusual understanding. "Pamela, if you feel that way about him, you're not ready for this." Beauty leant forward. "Are you sure you want to do this?"

"Feel what about him?" Pamela said, blinking rapidly.

"Jealousy," Beauty said simply. Ama came back with a tray laden with a sandwich and juice. She sat opposite Pamela, her eyes moving from one to the other. Pamela mumbled her thanks and started to eat. After a while, she put down the sandwich.

"I feel a lot of things where Mandla is concerned. I feel love, passion, compassion, hate, hurt, shame, and failure. I feel a whole lot of things, but that does not mean I don't want out. You can love a person only so much," she said, picking up the sandwich again.

"Okay," Beauty said, giving Pamela a wan smile. "From this point on we're going to hustle. Everything will depend on his reaction. But the point is for you, Pamela, to remain safe. And Ama, if Mandla comes here looking for Pam, let Lazaro answer the door." The ladies nodded their heads to show consent.

"After you're done, Pamela, we'll go."

"Go where?"

"To my house."

Beauty's house wasn't her first choice, but at that moment it seemed like the safest place there was.

"I'll drive you," Ama said, her voice sounding desperate. The other two women looked at her quizzically.

Not for the first time, Pamela wondered what was going on between her and Lazaro.

"Are you finished, Pam? I think I'll go and fetch my keys." Ama walked away without waiting for a response.

The hour was already going on seven. Mandla would be beside himself that she had disappeared without a word of explanation.

Ama returned with her keys and a very strange look on her face.

"Ama, are you alright?" Beauty asked. Ama's eyes slid from Beauty to Pamela, who was standing slightly behind Beauty.

"I'll be fine. Don't worry about me. Let's just get Pamela safe. Who knows: Mandla might be on his way here."

The drive to Beauty's house was tense. When they got there, the house was lit up like a Christmas tree. Beauty gave a satisfied sigh. It was truly pleasing to see the house alive again. She got out and waited for the others to follow.

"You know, I've never met your mother before," Pamela said.

"Well, you'll meet her today." Beauty said. Now she was alright with people meeting her mother and drawing their conclusions, which was what they'd already been doing without meeting her anyway. Life was funny. You hid for so long from the scrutiny of people only to find out that they scrutinise all the same. Beauty opened the front door, ushering in Pamela and Ama.

"Ma, there are some people here to see you!" she called, looking down the hall.

"Beauty," she replied in her sing-song voice.

"Come, we'll be in the sitting room." Beauty showed them the way. At the same time, her mother came shuffling through the sitting-room door. All eyes turned towards her. Pamela's reaction was the usual – she seemed unable to breath, swallow or look away. Ama took it in her stride. She looked over the disfigured creature that was Beauty's mother, and seemed to see nothing that was appalling or scary, her eyes registering only the pleasant interest of meeting a new person.

"Ma, this is Pamela and Ama."

"It's very nice to meet you." Her mother said, her eyes pausing on Ama. She shuffled across the room to take a seat.

"Pamela is going to be staying with us for a while," Beauty said.

"Oh." She sounded surprised, but quickly added. "You're welcome." Her eyes kept straying to Ama as she spoke.

"Ma, you're scaring her. Stop staring," Beauty said looking at her mother.

"No, she's not," Ama said. Steadily, she returned Beauty mother's stare.

"I've been meaning to ask how you're doing," Beauty's mother said tentatively.

"I'm fine." Ama gave her a weak smile.

"She means about Thabo," Beauty said. She guessed Ama had been thinking about Mandla and their plan. She noticed how at the mention of Thabo's name Ama seemed to wince slightly.

"I'm fine," Ama repeated, looking at Beauty.

"I heard you're living with his brother?" Beauty's mother continued.

"Yes."

"And he's not married."

"Yes." Ama's eyes came back to Beauty's mother.

"That was very kind of them," Beauty's mother nodded her head, as though confirming what she had said in her own mind.

"Ma!" Beauty shook her head.

"Kind of who?" Ama asked, frowning.

"Thabo's parents of course," Beauty's mother said, ignoring her daughter. "They gave you their son."

"They didn't have to do this. I could have lived on my own." Ama said.

"Yes, you could have. At least at the moment there's someone taking care of you."

"I didn't want someone to take care of me."

"Even so, he's keeping away stigma and the sly words of people out there from hurting you."

"Ma! Can we change the topic?"

But her mother continued. "Do you know that when your father left us there were talks? Before I could even heal, people were whispering about me, speculating about what could have turned him away. A man doesn't up and leave. They used to say that there had to be something wrong with me. And see," she said, pointing to her burnt skin, "there was something. He even tried to burn it out of me."

"The situations are not the same, Ma. My father didn't die. He was a vicious and cruel man, and it doesn't matter what they say out there." Beauty pointed towards the door.

"Oh, baby, but it does. Why do you think we've lived in this house shut away from the world for so long?"

"That won't happen to Ama." Annoyed, Beauty got to her feet. "Come, Ama, I'll see you to the door."

"No wait. I have a question." Ama turned Beauty's mother. "So you mean Lazaro is saving me from people out there?"

"In a way, yes."

"So I'm supposed to stay with him until I die, even though there's nothing between us? Even though I don't love him?"

Now Beauty's mother just stared at Ama. She looked bewildered, as if she couldn't believe that Ama was asking her such a question, and she should know better.

"I think I've read somewhere that love is a state of mind. If you change the way your mind sees things, the rest will follow. It starts with you."

"Are you telling me I should fall in love with Lazaro?" Ama seemed appalled at the idea.

"No."

"Then what?" Her voice rose. Pamela flinched in her seat. Beauty paced to the door. The conversation had gone on long enough. But she couldn't seem to stop her mother.

"All I'm saying is that life is what you make it. No one can decide for you. You choose what you want. And since you've lived with this Lazaro for so long, I'd say you know what you want."

"No, I don't." Ama's voice wavered. "This is not the way I pictured my life."

"Well, this is not the way I pictured my life either." Beauty's mother slowly got to her feet.

Beauty hung her head, letting her mother's words sink in. Before, her mind had been empty of any thoughts or hopes for her future. She hadn't dared see anything there, until Jeffrey.

"I think I'll say goodnight. It was nice to meet you all." Beauty's mother made her way slowly out of the room.

Sighing, Beauty turned to Ama. "Come, I'll take you to your car. Pamela, I won't be long. Please, make yourself at home while I'm gone."

Beauty followed Ama out of the room. Things seemed to be getting worse.

Chapter 20

It was Sunday and things were indeed getting worse. Pamela woke up feeling disorientated and out of sorts. It took her a while to figure out where she was, and her finding out she was in Beauty's house was not reassuring. The knowledge of it dragged her deeper into a state of self-pity. What woman would let such a state befall her? Pamela kept asking herself as she readied for work. Mandla had not called, and Pamela had kept looking at her phone, as though she could make it ring. His silence was getting to her. She wondered what he was thinking. Why was he not reacting to her leaving him? Didn't she mean anything to him? She moved through the motions of getting ready and eating breakfast. Beauty was there, preparing a tray of food to take to her mother.

Pamela could not help dwelling on the fact that Mandla didn't care about her. She felt forlorn at the thought, so much so that the moment her phone beeped she lunged for it, hoping it was Mandla. It was a message from him. Pamela felt an uncharacteristic feeling surge within her. She couldn't wait to find out what he'd said. For a second, she hoped he wanted her back, and longed for words of love and remorse in his message. But there were none. Pamela gasped in shock at the words of retribution typed there. It was as though he had slapped her all over again. Pamela stared at the screen of her phone, the words sinking in, and her hope faltered. How could she be so stupid?

"What is it, Pam?" Beauty asked, coming to her side. Pamela thrust the phone into Beauty's hands. Beauty quickly scanned the screen. "Oh! This is good. The angrier he gets, the better. The plan is working!" Beauty clapped her hands.

"Beauty, this is not a game. Like he said in the SMS, he's going to kill me!" Pamela's voice shook.

"Don't worry about it, Pam. You just go to work, and we'll take care of Mandla."

Pamela nodded. This is not a game, she thought to herself as she gathered her handbag, trying to gain some composure. She was strong, she told herself. It was just that sometimes her determination deserted her. She loved Mandla, there was no denying that. But she couldn't live like this anymore. She'd win her freedom; even if death was her freedom, she'd take it.

All this affirmed in her mind, Pamela made her way to work. She got on her bus, plastered a smile upon her face, and allowed words long committed to her memory flow in her melodic voice, conjuring a lifetime of experience and memories for those who listened. Even with the tourists' gleeful and attentive faces, Pamela couldn't shake the feeling of apprehension. In the back of her mind, she expected Mandla to show up at one of the tourist sites to bring to reality his words. Pamela felt restless, and as the day went on her edginess became worse. By the time her tour was over, she was feeling thoroughly unsettled, constantly on the lookout for Mandla. Even after she alighted from the bus at her offices, Pamela was vigilant – she hastily scanned the perimeter for any sign of him. Maybe he is trying to scare me into coming back, Pamela thought as she went inside to wait for her next shift. Or maybe he meant what he said; Mandla didn't make idle threats. She was growing more anxious with every step. She should cool down. She was scaring herself for nothing, Pamela thought. There was still an afternoon to get through – it was no good scaring herself witless. To succeed, she had to sustain herself, stay strong and focus on her goal: freedom. Pamela was so deep in thought that she didn't see her boss rush towards her. When his voice reached her ears close by, she almost jumped out of her skin.

"Pamela! There you are. Sorry, I didn't mean to scare you. Come along to my office, I'd like to have a chat." Pamela followed, still rattled.

"I've been worried about you," he said leaning back in his chair behind his desk. He looked genuinely concerned.

"Sibanyone, is something wrong?"

"No, no, no, it's just that your husband was here. He ..." Her boss cleared his throat and looked about him, somewhat nervous. His eyes scanned Pamela's face. Maybe he was looking for bruises, Pamela thought, but she wasn't sure. Over the years he'd witnessed a few – the ones Pamela hadn't been able to conceal. Pamela looked away from his inquisitive eyes.

"Is there anything wrong at home, Pamela? You would tell me if there was, wouldn't you?" Now he was fidgeting, clearing his throat again, as though he wished to take back his last question.

"Did he say something?" Pamela felt her stomach contract. Sibanyone watched her for a long while. She wondered if he could see her discomfort.

Their plan was working, but for some reason she wasn't feeling good about it.

"No, Pam. I don't believe there is any reason for us to rehash it. I just wanted to know you are okay. And I was thinking of giving you the rest of the day off. Mary will cover for you. She's already on her way here. I'll see you tomorrow, Pam. Go and fix whatever it is that's bothering your husband."

"Okay," Pamela said. She felt limp where she stood. Things were happening so fast, she couldn't even breathe. Pamela turned and walked out of the office. This was what she had wanted. Pamela's face contorted in pain at the thought. This was the beginning of attaining her freedom. She couldn't go back now – this was it. But why wasn't she feeling anything? There was no joy or exhilaration in celebration of their plan coming together. Mandla was reacting the way they had anticipated and wanted. Yet still, she couldn't feel anything. She was numb all over. Maybe she was still in shock at the prospect of seeing Mandla after just walking out on him yesterday.

Pamela walked through to the locker room she shared with her colleagues. Mechanically, she collected her belongings. She looked at her cellphone: there were no missed calls or messages. Maybe she should call Sizwe, she thought, looking at the screen. She frowned, staring down at it. What would she say to him? By now Mandla must have told him things she couldn't counter, even if she tried. Her son must believe she was a selfish woman who had abandoned them by now. Shoving the phone into her handbag, Pamela quickly walked out the office. She felt like she was standing outside of herself and everything was happening to her without her wanting it. I want this, Pamela told herself over and over in her mind, until it became a reality.

At the kerb she hailed a taxi. But as her fingers formed the signs that indicated Meadowlands Zone 5, she couldn't help but feel like she was taking the wrong taxi. Around her a bevy of hawkers, commuters and taxis milled about, she stepped around products laid out on the streets and pavements. Kliptown surged with life, and she felt like she was suffocating. Pamela felt a throbbing pressure in her brain. She released a sigh – she wanted this. And nothing was ever easy, she told herself. There'd come a day when she'd be proud of herself. And this day would mark the start of her life, Pamela thought, but she wasn't sure if she believed herself.

After a long series of blinking robots and twisting turns, she arrived at Beauty's house to find her bustling about in her hair salon. Even though it was still early in the day, the salon was full of people wanting their hair done. Maybe they saw something wonderful in their future that they felt they should prepare for, Pamela thought. She couldn't remember the last time she'd had her hair done. Now she went about with short, easy-to-maintain hair. Plus this meant that Mandla had fewer things on her body to grab on. A memory of herself with freshly braided hair being dragged along the tiled floor of her home popped into her mind.

Pamela turned away from the salon and made her way to the front door. She walked through to the sitting room. Beauty's mother was nowhere in sight, and Pamela was relieved. She couldn't see herself being able to converse with Beauty's mother at that moment. The woman had an annoying way of seeing the truth and having no qualms about voicing it. She could cut right through a person. Last night she'd spoken a truth that Pamela couldn't deny: she'd said that life was what you made it. If that was so, Pamela felt she had failed miserably. She had done nothing but dig herself deeper into the abyss she now loathed to leave. Why was that, Pamela asked herself. Why was she suddenly reluctant to leave Mandla, even though she knew she couldn't go back? He'd kill her before he let her go.

Pamela sunk onto a sofa. Pamela mulled the question over in her mind until she didn't want to think anymore. She just wanted a moment of silence and a respite from everything. Closing her eyes, she prayed for the strength she knew she'd need.

"Pam, I thought you'd come through to the salon." Beauty interrupted her hard won peace. Pamela abruptly opened her eyes.

"I just wanted a moment to myself," she said, sitting up straight.

"Are you okay?" Beauty said, coming closer.

"I'm fine." She closed her eyes for a moment. "Mandla went to see my boss. He didn't tell me what they talked about, but I have a feeling he wasn't just looking for me."

"He came to your office?"

Pamela nodded.

"And where were you?"

"I was still working."

"And you came here straight afterwards?"

"Yes," Pamela said, confused.

"Shit!" Beauty said spinning around. Pamela's eyes rounded, her fear becoming a reality.

"This is what we wanted, isn't it?" Pamela asked, feeling her fear burn her gut. If Mandla got his hands on her now he'd make sure she paid dearly for making a fool of him.

"Yes, it is. But there is one problem. You came straight here after hearing he was at your office. He could have easily waited for you to return from your tour and followed you. By the way, why are you here so early? I thought you had a double shift."

"My boss gave me the day off." Now Pamela's eyes were ready to pop out of their sockets.

"Why?"

"He wanted me to fix whatever is bothering Mandla."

"Why didn't he tell you what Mandla said?"

"I don't know. Beauty, you're scaring me. This is what we wanted to achieve: he's going mad. And people know about it. Oh, my God …" Pamela's hands flew to her lips. Tears gathered in her eyes "He's going to kill me. At the end of it all, that's what is going to happen to me," she said, nodding her head as though confirming the fact to herself.

"Let's not get ahead of ourselves. Maybe he's cleverer than I thought. Let's not panic. We just have to be a step ahead of him." Beauty sat down next to Pamela. "Okay, let's assume he's followed you here. There are two options. Number one: he comes here hollering and causing a racket, because he wants you back, in which case we call the police. I'll do the talking and you'll substantiate whatever I say, which will be more proof against him. Number two: if he's a sadistic son of a bitch, which I believe he is, he'll bide his time and wait for the right moment to strike, which means we have to change our plan slightly?" Beauty turned to look at Pamela. She nodded.

"You have to invite him to lunch tomorrow. Ama already has some Valium to spike his drink."

"What?"

"You'll call him tomorrow and tell him you want to talk, but that you'd feel safer at a public place. And then you can spill something, ask him to get you a napkin, and while he's gone you spike his drink. I'll be there with you, Pam. And I think it's time you called your son and explained some things to him. He's old enough, I think he'll understand your wanting to be free from his father. And also ask him to take the children somewhere after school. We'll pick them up later." Beauty softened her tone. "Whatever happens tonight, we'll be waiting for him. Don't worry, I won't let him hurt you." Beauty squeezed Pamela's hand. "I have to go back to the salon. Call your son. We'll see what happens tomorrow."

Pamela watched Beauty leave. She felt so alone, despite what her friends were doing to try to help her. She was still in this alone. She felt defeated before she'd even begun. It was as though Mandla were beating her all over again, stripping her of her will and strength. Fishing around in her handbag, she found her cellphone. Pamela pushed a few buttons, and then waited for the call to connect.

Ama watched the clock on the cubicle wall toil away. It was some minutes past midday. The ward was quiet as patients slept their medicated systems into some semblance of health, but the quietness was interrupted here and there by the comings and goings of her fellow nurses. Ama sat at her table half listening to their lively talk. Every so often Ama's ear registered the high-pitched voice of one of her colleagues. It was Nelly. She reminded Ama so much of Matlakala. There was no facial resemblance. It was the way Nelly viewed the world that was so similar to Matlakala's outlook. Thinking about her friend, she sighed. What a waste.

Ama's eyes shifted from the clock to the table, thinking about Lazaro's request. Last night after her brief visit at Beauty's house, Ama had felt out of sorts. Her heart ached until she couldn't bear the pain or stop her tears. She had stood there at the front door, barely within the threshold, watching Lazaro watch her, concern written in his eyes, his feet carrying him towards her. And when his arms came around her, she'd cried and he had held on. After she had spent all her tears, she'd pushed away from him. She didn't want any comfort from him. Lazaro wasn't the man of her choosing, so there was no reason to think of him as being anything to her.

After their awkward embrace, Lazaro had produced something from his trouser pocket.

"I'd like you to go somewhere with me," he said taking hold of her hand and placing a piece of paper in her palm.

It was a complementary ticket to a gallery opening. Ama hadn't known what to say, and Lazaro hadn't waited for any answer. He left her there at the threshold to make up her mind. It was her choice whether she went home early enough to make the time the opening was due to start.

Now, Ama's eyes went back to the clock. She still had time to decide. She shoved the ticket into her bag. In the next hour the doctors would be making their rounds, so she needed to prepare for that. Getting up she adjusted her uniform and returned to work. This was what she knew best. It required only her expertise and care. As she moved about, she immersed herself in the caring for others. And when rounds began, she watched as the doctors checked on the progress of their patients, prescribed new or more medication, unwound bandages and brandished syringes, leaving the ward in a mess that Ama and her colleagues would have to tidy.

When Ama thought to look at the clock it was time to make a decision. She stood there watching the hands turn. What was the worst that could happen? Life was what one made it, after all, Ama thought. She couldn't live with pain for the rest of her life. Even the hate she felt for Pamela's husband wouldn't keep her going for long. She had to start living her life.

On impulse, she spun around and went to find the unit manager to ask to leave early. She hadn't been amongst the nurses scurrying behind the doctors during their rounds, so went to look for her in their cubicle, where Nelly was entertaining some of the nurses with one of her love stories, but she wasn't there either. Ama thought of going to her friend Matron Makgoba, but decided against it. She didn't want to start any office politics, and she was already the source of some gossip. She would have to ask Nelly to cover for her.

"What, you have a date?" The subject of men was never far from Nelly's mind.

"No, it's nothing like that." Ama gathered her belongings. It wouldn't be good if that's what Lazaro had in mind. What would everyone think of her gallivanting about with her dead husband's brother? Maybe it wasn't about everyone, Ama thought. She took a breath, not wanting to think about it.

"It wouldn't be a bad thing, Ama. Every woman needs a man. No matter how hard we try to pretend we don't."

"A friend of mine used to say that. You remind me of her," Ama said, readying to leave. "I'll see you tomorrow, Nelly, and thanks."

Ama walked out of the ward. She didn't know if she was doing the right thing. She wondered what Matlakala would have said about Lazaro. Maybe not much, except that everyone deserved love regardless of where it came from. But Lazaro didn't love her, and she didn't love him. Love was a state of mind, someone had written somewhere. And now she, Ama, was confusing herself, because deep down she craved something that was forever beyond her reach. Or was it?

"Go now, before it gets late," Nelly said with a soft expression on her face.

"Thank you," Ama said again, her decision made.

"Be sure to tell me about it. That will be thanks enough for me." Ama felt laughter rising within her at Nelly's words. If only she knew: this was nothing close to being a date. But who knows, Ama thought, feeling suddenly slightly giddy and happy. She felt wanted. Ama walked through the double doors with a spring in her step. Just outside the door Ama almost collided with her unit manager talking to some other managers. Before they spotted her Ama was able to catch a few words of their hushed conversation.

"No I haven't heard that," one of them said. "It's true: they say women like that, if they ever have a man, he'll die."

Another said, "What's wrong with these women?"

Ama gasped at the words, knowing very well they were speaking about her. Her gasp caught their attention. They stopped their conversation and turned her way, looking guilty. Ama gathered herself and prepared to face her unit manager. It wasn't her fault that Thabo had decided to kill himself, leaving her behind to be viewed as unworthy of any man. With one stroke, she was not fit to be a woman.

Ama straightened her spine.

"Could I please go home early? I have somewhere I need to be." Ama looked directly into the woman's eyes. Her unit manager squirmed, mumbling some form of consent.

"Thank you," Ama said, stepping around them on the narrow paved pathway. She quickly made her way to her car. The joviality she'd felt a few minutes earlier waned. She wondered why happiness in her life was so short-lived.

Ama got into her car and drove off.

When she got home, she found Lazaro waiting for her in the sitting room, dressed in his Sunday best. He really made a handsome picture. His face was blank as usual, but Ama could see through that now. She was getting used to him. Their eyes locked, and Ama could see that he was grateful that she had come. Somewhat shy beneath his scrutiny, she took a few steps towards her room.

"I'll go and change," she told him, looking away. Lazaro just nodded and took a seat, resuming his wait.

In her room, Ama quickened her movements. She breezed through a lukewarm shower to get the hospital smell off of her. She didn't want to consider her appearance and pulled on the first thing she found in her cupboard. Lazaro and she were nothing, she thought, there was not need to make an effort.

As she was fixing her hair, Ama's phone rang. It was Jeffrey. She felt a rush of affection at the sound of his voice. She missed him.

"How are you? I haven't seen you around for a while. What's up?" Ama said, running a hand through her hair. She needed a visit to the salon – get some relaxer in there to straighten the natural springs out. Her hair still looked good, but some TLC wouldn't hurt.

"Hi, sis. I know. I've been busy." Jeffrey sounded evasive to Ama's ears.

"You went back to work?"

"Yes, it was about time. So how are things on your side?"

"They're okay."

"And Lazaro?"

Ama paused, thinking honesty was the best policy at that moment. "He's fine, and he's invited me to a gallery opening."

"Oh …" Jeffrey said. Ama sensed disapproval in his voice. He was just like the others.

"Oh what?" Ama said. "Shouldn't he have?"

An unnerving silence followed her question.

"Jeffrey?"

"You can do whatever you want, Ama."

"You're sounding like Lazaro is a mistake, Jeffrey. Yet you allowed them to palm me off on him. Where did you think all this would end up? Anyway, to put your mind at ease, he's just taking me to watch a stupid gallery opening, nothing more. I still have to comb my hair. I'll talk to you later." Ama suddenly felt very tired. It was debilitating not knowing which path to take. And if ever she did choose, how would she know which path would be acceptable in the eyes of those who bothered to see and condemn? If only Thabo was still alive, if only things had gone her way ... Ama wouldn't allow her mind to venture into that direction. Tonight she'd try to be happy, at peace.

"I don't know what to say to you, Ama. Yes, I allowed it. But now ... Do you like him, Ama? Just be honest with me, sis." He cleared his throat. "It's not a bad thing."

"I ... I haven't really thought about it."

"You haven't?"

"No."

"Okay, well just know that it's not a bad thing. Even if you want someone out there, you can, you know? You're not dead, Ama, Thabo is. You have every right to live your life."

"I understand, Jeffrey. Thanks. When are you coming over? I'd like to see you." Ama reached for her comb.

"I'll let you know when I have time. Goodnight, Ama. Enjoy yourself –"

"Wait. Jeffrey?"

"What?"

"Beauty, you haven't spoken about her. Is something wrong?"

Ama heard Jeffrey sigh. "That's a story for another day. Goodnight, Ama."

"Night," Ama said, staring at herself in the mirror. She took in her dark skin, her plain face, and came to a decision. After she and her friends gave Mandla his medicine, and he'd swallowed it, tasting its bitter taste, she'd take off the invincible mourning garb she'd worn for Thabo and move on with her life. And she would not let what people said get to her, especially the women. She wouldn't be the first or the last to be judged.

"I'm going to live my life," Ama said to the empty room. With that in her mind, she quickly combed her hair. Lazaro must be getting impatient by now. Finished, Ama rushed into the sitting room to find him still waiting patiently.

"I'm ready," she said, watching him stand. He was quieter than usual, but Ama was grateful for his calm silence on the way to the gallery. The show was being held in the entertainment district of Newtown. Ama had let Lazaro drive, and she watched him park the car alongside a welcomingly lit building. People were already milling about outside, creating a festive atmosphere. This was life, Ama thought, getting out of the car and making her way towards the lights.

Lazaro came to her side, guiding her to the entrance of the reception area. The show had not started yet, because the double doors leading to the main gallery were still closed. Once inside, Lazaro turned to her.

"I have to do something, I'll be right back."

Ama stayed behind in the crowds gathered outside the closed doors, soaking in their laughter and sense of anticipation. This was life, she thought again.

Suddenly, the double doors opened, revealing another spectacularly lit room. The crowd produced their tickets and were shown inside. Enraptured, Ama walked forward, Lazaro forgotten.

Inside, there were paintings hung and lit at the random angles and random spaces. A well-dressed man welcomed everyone, saying how pleased he was with the turnout that evening. He ended off introducing the artist. Lazaro stepped forward to address his audience. Ama listened to his voice. He sounded different, more animated than she'd heard him before.

"I'd like to thank everyone for coming. And especially Victor," he turned to the well-dressed man, "whose nagging finally paid off." He smiled.

Ama had never seen him like this.

"Anyway, I'm glad he did. Thank you, Victor. When he first approached me I didn't have a collection in mind. I painted what I felt and what I saw happening around me. The paintings are pieces of my life. I hope you enjoy them," he finished off, his eyes going in search of Ama. Soothing music came from above, creating a rhythm that the audience followed as they moved from one painting to the other.

Lazaro joined Ama. "Would you like me to show you the paintings?"

"Of course."

He took her arm, and led her to the nearest piece.

It was of a black woman balancing two young children on rounded hips, which were wrapped in a cloth with an ethnic design. She held the children there so effortlessly, the strength in her arms and stature evident in every stroke of the brush. She looked unshakable – firm and planted deep into the ground. Her black skin appeared rough and weathered, much like the soil she stood on. As Ama looked at her, the image of a baobab tree came to mind.

"So you've been doing this for a long time," she said, moving to the next painting.

"Yes." Lazaro followed her.

"This is nice," she said, looking at a landscape. The scene depicted on the canvas was wild, open, fresh. The horizon seemed endless. "It's almost as though you've lived there," Ama said.

They moved on to the next painting. When Ama laid eyes on it, it was as though she was looking into a mirror.

"This is me."

"Yes."

"Why am I crying with only one eye?" she asked, turning towards him.

"I don't know, maybe that's how I see you."

"What do you mean?"

Instead of answering her, Lazaro gently pushed her forward to another painting. This one held Thabo's image along with the baobab-like woman and her two children. They made a nice-looking family. Thabo smiled happily at the woman, his face showing his joy, and love. Ama stared, not daring to ask the questions that were flooding her mind. The more she stared, the more she could see the resemblance between Thabo and the children. Lazaro was truly a talented painter.

"Thabo had a family before you," Lazaro said. Ama stared at the painting one last time, and then turned for the double doors. Lazaro waited for a few seconds before following her outside.

She had managed to reach her car and was standing beside it, her back to him. Head bowed, Ama felt warm tears splash her face. She heard Lazaro behind her.

"So I was the other woman?" she asked, without turning around. She leant against the car, feeling dizzy.

"Yes."

"Why didn't anyone tell me?"

"Because at the time it wasn't our place."

The sick feeling in her stomach turned to anger. "Bullshit! Don't give me that. He's been dead for months, and no one thought to tell me! Why not? Did they think they could just pass you on to me, because no one else would have you? That I should not hope for any better. Is that it?"

"No. My parents were trying to make it up to you."

"So you all thought I was some kind of pity case then? Meanwhile all along I was really the other woman! I stole Thabo from another woman. Do you think that needs rewarding?" Ama wanted to scream or hit someone, preferably Lazaro. How could they not tell her this? She would have broken it off with Thabo the minute she knew. What kind of woman did this make her now?

"Don't blame yourself, Ama. You didn't know," Lazaro said. "I know you're angry, Ama, but it doesn't really matter now, because you can't change the past. What's happened has happened. Thabo is gone. All I wanted was for you to know. You asked me why I painted you weeping with one eye. It's because I see so much in your future, but no matter what life brings your way, you keep looking behind you with one eye, as if you lost something back there. But you didn't. That something was never yours to begin with."

"That's easy for you to say."

"Thabo met Emma years before he met you," Lazaro continued. "He loved her, had two kids by her, and he wanted to marry her, but our parents didn't approve of her because she was from Zimbabwe. She was different and they didn't think she suited their son, but Thabo wanted her and only her, which meant that he'd upset and disappoint our parents, and that was something he never wanted to do. In everything he did, he strived to please them: through his work, achievements, everything." Lazaro looked away from Ama. "You see, my brother had a lot to make up for, because of me. They would take me from one specialist to the next. At one point they thought it might be Asperger's."

"That's a type of autism, isn't it?" Ama said, remembering the rumours.

"Yeah, something like that" Lazaro said. He sounded like he didn't like the label. "It was difficult. My parents could never understand me, why I behaved differently, why I couldn't interact with others, why my progress was sometimes slower than others. They tried their best to make me normal, but I wasn't and never did improve. Then Thabo was born. And he took the place of firstborn. He did well, and never disappointed them: until Emma. So to please my parents, he met you, paid lobola for you, and there was the wedding ceremony in the church." He turned to Ama then. "I guess he thought he could keep you both. With you, he could please our parents, and with Emma he could have his life."

Tears choked Ama. So Thabo had never wanted her. The truth of it was hard to bear. Suddenly Ama wanted to go home, the home where her parents had wanted her and loved her.

"He would have married her the traditional way eventually. Polygamy is legal in this country."

"If he had it all figured out, then why did he kill himself?"

"Emma found out. She didn't want anything to do with him. I think she had been hurt and humiliated so much by my parents already, and this was the final straw."

"Good for her," Ama said. "Could I have my keys please? I think I've heard enough."

Lazaro took a few steps closer to her. "I'm sorry, Ama."

"Don't be sorry, you didn't do anything wrong." She looked at him, her hand still stretched out for her keys. Lazaro fished them out of his pocket and gently placed them into her hand.

"If you knew this about your brother, why did you agree to your parents burdening you with me? Don't you think they were controlling you, as they did him?" Lazaro stared at her, his face blank as ever, but Ama noted how she didn't have to look for any expression on his face to know what he was feeling. Then and there she saw and felt what she had been too scared to acknowledge. Thabo wasn't here anymore – it was just Lazaro and her looking at each other, wondering how to live the life they shared. Ama looked away.

"Like your brother said, I was helping you get through your grief …"

"I was never your responsibility," Ama interrupted.

"I didn't say you were. But a man can take care of a woman if he wants to. And it has been my pleasure, Ama." His right hand suddenly came out to softly graze her cheek. Ama felt air catch in her chest.

"You'll have the house to yourself by tomorrow. Drive safely," Lazaro said and then disappeared into the throng of excited people making their way into the gallery. Ama stared after him. Life was not fair – it was not fair. She got into her car and started the engine.

What was she supposed to do? How was she to live her life so that the things she wanted would come to her? She had mourned a man who hadn't wanted her – she had felt his rejection in his death, even though she hadn't known how deep that rejection was. Suddenly she felt afraid, afraid of the possibilities proving to be impossibilities. Ama's tears fell, her vision blurred, and she held onto the steering wheel. Possibilities. Lazaro and her together: it was a possibility, but then he was moving out, which made the whole thing impossible, plus he was there under some obligation to his brother and family. As Ama drove, she felt a sense of calm begin to take over. Maybe it was time she learnt to accept things as they were.

She made a turn, taking the route to Beauty's house. Before long she was parked at Beauty's front gate. The lights of the house were blazing. Ama wondered why they switched on so many lights. Weren't they worried about the electricity bill, or global warming for that matter? Ama made her way to the front door. She knocked once, and the door flew open.

"You look terrible," Beauty said her voice showing little sympathy. But Ama knew she cared in her own way.

"I know."

"What did Lazaro do?" Beauty asked, letting Ama in.

"Must it have something to do with a man?"

"If it was something else you would have told me before I even asked." They went into the sitting room where Pamela had not moved since she'd returned from work. Ama went to sit beside Pamela. She was relieved that Mandla hadn't caused Thabo's suicide: that was one thing positive about this night. Ama hugged Pamela close with one arm.

"Where is your mother?" Ama asked Beauty, looking around.

"Don't worry, she won't bother you today. She's in her room busy with something."

"What does she do? Doesn't she get lonely?" Ama asked, not sure she could bear a life of solitude, especially forced solitude. She wanted someone. She wanted someone to love her, always.

"She reads, mostly. As for whether she gets lonely, I think she's made peace with her life, and she enjoys her own company more than anyone else's."

"I don't think I could ever get used to that." Ama patted Pamela's arm "You're awfully quiet, Pam, are you okay?" Pamela gave Ama a wan smile, but did not answer.

"Did you manage to find the people I asked you to find?" Beauty asked.

"Yes, I did. Sizwe is happy about my decision."

"Is he?" Beauty sounded surprised.

"You told him, Pam? That's … that's wonderful. I think. At least one person is happy about the changes that are happening."

"I'll get used to it, Beauty. It won't happen overnight."

"The only thing that scares me …" Beauty became silent, thinking over her words "The only thing that scares me is that maybe you feel we're forcing you. And maybe this is not what you want, maybe you haven't thought it through. If you feel that way, Pamela, after everything, when you are divorced and have to face life alone, you'll hate us, not Mandla, but Ama and I. It's difficult. I know. But it has to be something you want. Pamela, this …" Tears filled Beauty's eyes.

"Beauty?"

"I'm fine, Ama. I just don't want to do this only to find out that Pamela is having second thoughts."

"Are you having second thoughts, Pam?" Ama asked, wondering what would happen if Pamela were indeed having second thoughts. She wanted Mandla to pay for what he was doing to her friend. What was going to happen?

"We're not going to kill him," Pamela said looking at both of them.

"No, we're not." Beauty said.

"What are you thinking, Pam?"

"I don't know, Ama! I just don't feel right doing anything to him."

"Okay … But you can't go back to him, you know that, don't you?" Ama was horrified. "He'll kill you, Pam."

"I know that." Pamela said, looking down at her clasped hands. To Ama, it looked like the whole world was weighing her down.

"Pamela, I don't mean to judge you, but this is crazy, if not suicidal! You can't …"

"Ama, it's okay. Let her be. She has decided," said Beauty.

"Don't you dare say that. We haven't even begun to know that we have lost. Pam, this is completely insane, and you know it!" Ama felt like she was going crazy herself.

"I don't think … Goodness." Pamela got to her feet. Tears were streaming down her face. "You have to understand, Beauty, Ama. I'm not giving up. I'm just … I'm just …"

Suddenly there was a commotion at the front door. Pamela's name was being hollered for all to hear. A deafening banging followed, causing the door to rattle in its frame. It was a miracle that it held. Instantly, the women got to their feet. They had to do something, Ama thought.

"He's here," Pamela said, stating the obvious. She wrung her hands as fear coursed through her, her eyes anxiously on the door.

"Don't worry, I'll call the police," Beauty said, searching for her phone.

"Pamela!" Her name was barked out again.

"This has gone on for too long," Ama said, moving towards the kitchen.

"No, Ama! We don't know what he wants."

"Of course we do." Ama looked at Beauty.

"Beauty!" another agitated voice added to the din Mandla was making.

"Everything is fine, Ma. I'm calling the police. Stay in your room." Beauty frantically searched for her cellphone. She looked beneath cushions and under the sofa, eventually finding it hidden under a throw. Having found the number for the police, she waited for the call to connect.

"Wait!" Pamela said, her eyes still dilated, her fear palpable. Ama and Beauty turned to her, astounded.

"No, Pam, we talked about this. Everything will be over tomorrow." Beauty said, her voice already resigned to the inevitable. The three women silently stared at each other. Mandla went on pounding at the door, shouting obscenities.

"This is my problem. I shouldn't have involved you. Don't worry, I'll be fine." Pamela gave them a wobbly smile and picked up her bag. "I'll come for my other stuff. Don't worry, I'll be fine."

"You don't have to convince us, Pam. Your loving husband is waiting," Beauty said, disconnecting the call. She sat down. At that moment, defeat was tangible. Ama watched Pamela walk out of the kitchen. Mandla continued with his rage-filled words, making sure everyone in the house could hear him. He ranted and he raved, then as quickly as he had come, he was gone.

Ama cast her eyes nervously towards the kitchen door. Pamela wouldn't make it through the night, but there was nothing they could do.

"He's going to kill her," Ama said.

"I know."

"And?"

"And we'll bury her and that will be the end of it. At least we won't have to worry about her. She'll be far away from that psycho."

"How can you say such a thing, Beauty? Don't you see what just happened?"

"I see, Ama."

"So, what? You don't care. He'll kill her if we don't do something."

"If you haven't noticed, Pamela doesn't want to do anything about her situation. And frankly I'm tired of thinking about her with that pig. Maybe you should go home, Ama."

"No! I'm not going to stand by and watch another woman die at the hands of a man. Like Matlakala. This time I won't let it happen. We have to help her."

"She doesn't want help, Ama."

"I don't care if she doesn't want it. Let's go." Ama grabbed Beauty's arm to pull her up.

"Think about it, Ama. What are we going to do when we get there? Mandla won't even let us through the front door. What then?"

"It's better than sitting here doing nothing, while we know he's killing her. You might not care, Beauty, but I do." She stalked off to where she had been sitting. Fishing for her cellphone in her handbag, she pressed a few buttons and waited for the call to connect. She spoke to police dispatch, answering questions and giving out Pamela's address. After the call, Ama faced Beauty.

"The police are on their way to her house." Her eyes did not waver as she spoke her next words. "And I'm going there as well. I know what the police can be like, so I think it's best that there's someone to protect Pamela until they arrive. But first I'm going to my house to fetch something to protect myself against that fool. This time is the last time he puts his hands on that woman, I don't care whether Pamela likes it or not." Ama swivelled to the door, and abruptly stopped. "You should learn to care more, Beauty. Caring is the only thing that makes this life worthwhile. It is the only thing that's pure within us, the only thing that is free, or should be free. Remember Jeffrey? He's still alive, Beauty. You can make amends and at least learn to care. It's never too late for that, believe me. I'm learning that the future is determined by today and not what we think of tomorrow." With that she was out the door.

"Ama, wait!" Beauty rushed to the front door. "Wait while I get some stuff. I won't take long." She dashed to her room.

Ama waited at the gate, glad that she won't have to face Mandla alone.

Chapter 21

On the way to Pamela's house, Ama tried not to imagine what they might find there. The darkness surrounding them as the car ploughed on made her feel as if they were the sole beings on that road. Ama had a moment of déjà vu, remembering the night Matlakala had died. At least that night Lazaro had been with her. He had been a silent pillar of support. Ama had somehow expected to see him at the house when she had gone there earlier to fetch the morphine and bandages, along with a wicked-looking knife, just in case. But he had been out.

Ama turned to Beauty.

"What's going to happen?" she asked. Her hands held on tightly to the steering wheel. Soon they'd arrive at Pamela's house. They needed to make a plan.

"It depends on what we find there."

Of course, Ama thought. She watched Beauty for a moment. She was clutching a black canvas bag to her bosom. Ama wondered what was inside it. She'd find out soon enough, Ama thought as Pamela's house came into view. Ama parked the car along the pavement, near the fence. From where they sat, the house looked peaceful.

"Are we going to knock at the front door?" Beauty said.

"I guess." Ama reached for the bag full of weapons on the back seat. "If she's okay, we're leaving."

"Of course. Then there wouldn't be any reason to stay."

"Will she ever leave him, do you think?"

"No. Not out of her own will." Beauty got out of the car and disappeared in the darkness. They approached the front door, their hands clutching tightly onto their bags, as though they were shields to protect them from the foe within. At the door they stood, not sure what to do.

"We're here, we might as well," Beauty said, quickly rapping on the door. If there was anything to be done for Pamela, it had to be now.

As though he had been waiting for them, the door swung open with such force it banged against the wall. It was Sizwe. He stood there, his eyes wild, like a caged animal. Shivering, his arms were wrapped around his body. Ama almost screamed when she saw the blood smeared all over his arms. Taking charge, Beauty shoved her way through the door. She scanned the immediate space, finding Pamela's youngest son, Sihle, cowering in a corner of the sitting room. Ama wondered where Njabulo was. Beauty went over to the boy and crouched down, placing a hand tentatively on his arm. Sihle shrunk away in fear. A tiny whimper escaped his small form.

"Where is your Njabulo?" she softly asked, trying to gently move him from the corner.

"Mamma …" he said, refusing to move.

"Where is she?"

Ama left Beauty with the child and began to make her way down the passage, towards the bedroom.

Looking inside the first one, she gasped in horror at what she saw, causing Beauty to rush to her side. She heard Beauty's sharp intake of breath. They stood there afraid to go to her, afraid to confirm what they were both thinking. Ama felt herself being dragged away from the doorway.

"Ama, call the police again and call an ambulance. After you're done, help Sizwe wash the blood off his arms. And find him some clean clothes. I'm going to find Njabulo." Before Beauty could turn towards the passageway Sizwe stopped her.

"He ran this way when everything started," he said, pointing to the kitchen. Beauty followed, leaving Ama still rooted to her spot.

"Make the call Ama!" she shouted before disappearing into the kitchen.

"Yes," Ama said as though waking up from a trance. She closed her eyes, but the image of Pamela's bloodied body lying just inside the open door of her bedroom wouldn't go away. She looked inside again, and she was still lying there, her arms outstretched, her head strained forward as though she were trying to crawl away but had died in her effort. From where she stood, Ama could see some of the disarray in the room, but there was no sign of Mandla. Turning away, she reached into her bag, found her phone and called for an ambulance, the police and her brother. Jeffrey picked up on the second ring.

"I think Pamela is dead," Ama said.

"What?"

"She's lying there, not moving, and there's blood everywhere. And I'm too afraid to go and check. I think she is dead." Ama shuddered and hurried to the sitting room, away from the horrific scene. Images of Matlakala's dead body ran in her mind. It happening again, she kept thinking.

"Ama, where are you?"

"At Pamela's house," she said, her eyes going to the boy in the corner. He still wouldn't move.

"Get out of the house, Ama, now! I'll be there as soon as I can." There was a pause "Where is Mandla?"

"I don't know," Ama said.

"Get out of the house. Do you hear me?"

"I have to go and find Beauty."

"She's there?"

"Yes, she's trying to find …"

"Get out of the house, I'm coming right now."

The line went dead. Ama debated what to do. She decided that there was nothing she could do in the house besides wait. She went to the little boy in the corner and scooped him up in her arms, holding on tight when he tried to struggle free. She rushed into the kitchen, looking for Beauty. At that moment Beauty came through the back door, Sizwe tailing her. He still looked terrified, but Ama could tell he was handling things better than she was.

"We can't find him," Beauty said, her voice strained.

"Jeffrey said he'd be here soon. He said we must get out of the house."

"No, Sizwe has to wash first …"

"How did you get that blood on you?"

Sizwe looked away from them. Maybe he shouldn't wash, Ama thought. It wouldn't help if the police found his discarded clothes and thought he was hiding something. Ama looked from Beauty to Sizwe. Maybe they were trying to hide something.

"Beauty?"

"Mandla is dead, Ama," Beauty said, moving towards the sink. An ashen Sizwe followed. He gave Beauty his hands. She scrubbed away, using more soap than necessary.

"How? What did Sizwe do?" At that moment she could hear sirens from outside. Vehicles came to a screeching halt and footsteps sounded, coming closer. They had left the door open. Ama turned towards the sitting room. Two paramedics rushed through. From where she stood, Ama heard the tap water cease. Beauty and Sizwe came forward, looking almost relaxed. But she knew they weren't.

"We've received an emergency call," one of the paramedics spoke.

"Yes, please come this way," Ama said, moving towards the bedroom. Beauty stopped to take the little boy from her arms. Ama led the paramedics along the passageway, but held back at the bedroom, watching them rush over to Pamela's still form.

Ama went back to the sitting room, leaving them to do their work. More cars came to a stop outside and within minutes two uniformed police officers walked through the door. They looked around. Ama pointed them to Pamela's room.

"I'm going to wait outside," Beauty said, still holding the boy. "We have to find your brother," she said to Sizwe, who nodded in response.

"He couldn't have gone far," Ama said.

"I don't know, but when someone is in shock anything is possible," she said, and then walked out the door. Ama followed them outside.

A policeman was approaching. He introduced himself as Detective Maja.

"I would like to ask you a few questions," he said. Sizwe looked nervously at the detective and then at Beauty. He looked like he was about to cry.

"Maybe the children could excuse us. I think they've been through enough," Ama said, turning to Detective Maja. More cars came to a halt outside the house, their doors slamming in unison as police officers and paramedics rushed to the scene. Ama saw Jeffrey get out of one of the cars. He rushed towards them.

"Maybe the little boy should be examined, but the older one can tell us what happened." The detective pointed to Sizwe. "You did say you came too late. So he's the only one who knows what happened."

"I thought what happened is very simple," Beauty was quick to say. "Mandla attacked Pam, and somehow she got the better of him and she bashed him with a bat."

"Were you in the room, ma'am?"

"Not at the time. But I saw the bat on the floor and put two and two together."

"I don't know what we're standing here for. Njabulo, their brother, is missing. He ran out of the house while his mother was being beaten to death. We have to go and look for him." Beauty shifted the boy in her arms to a better position. "Are you going to help us?"

"We will do that, but ..."

"We called your station before anything could happen to that woman in there. You took your time. We called again, you took your time and now you're wasting time. I'm going to look for that boy. Sizwe, take your brother to the ambulance." Beauty handed over Sihle to Sizwe. "Keys, Ama. I'll use your car."

"We'll use mine." Jeffrey said, stopping Ama. Jeffrey took hold of Beauty's arm and pulled her towards the gate. Ama turned and anxiously looked at the house. She hoped Pam was alright.

"So where do we start?" Jeffrey asked, starting the car.

"I don't know," she said, her eyes going to the ambulance at the gate. The paramedics were closing the doors. They were taking them to hospital. That was a good thing, Beauty thought; Sizwe would be far from the house. He'd have time to think things through.

"You have to think: where could a boy his age have run to?" Driving off the kerb, he glided along the tar road. They drove around for a while in silence. Here and there they spotted police vans circling the area near Pamela's home. Their blue lights shone bright, even at a distance.

"They're thinking he can't have gone far," Beauty said.

"And you think he has?"

"Fear is something else," she said quietly. She knew how fear could rule the senses, driving you over the edge.

"Sometimes fear can make you run and run until you don't have strength in your bones and all you can do is drag yourself along, because you're terrified of what's behind you, what might be coming for you. Other times, fear freezes you, and the only thing you can hear and feel is your heartbeat, the trembles that run through your body, the rushing of blood in your veins, yet you can't move. No matter what you try, you can't move."

"Beauty." Jeffrey placed his hands on her shoulders. She felt their warmth on her skin, and it took her a while to realise that he'd stopped the car, and was now looking at her with such compassion that she wanted to cry.

"Do you want to know the truth, Jeffrey? The truth is I have loved you from the first moment you hugged me at Orlando stadium. But I was scared to even think about what that meant. Scared to even …" Beauty sighed, letting out the pent-up fears she'd held within. "Even though it was a long time ago, I remember what happened as though it was only yesterday. The 13th of May 1999. It was around quarter to two in the afternoon. My mother says I wasn't supposed to be in the house. But I was there in the sitting room, hiding behind the sofa. I can't remember why. I saw him, my father. He was holding a see-through bottle filled with some colourless substance. I saw him sneaking through to the bedroom. He held the bottle close, opening the lid. From my hiding spot I remember wondering why were they so silent. Usually they came through making such a noise that Ma would have to shush them to be quiet. And then from the bedroom I heard my father shouting at my mother. Without thinking, I rushed into the room. I found her lying on the floor, writhing in pain and scratching at her face. When she saw me she screamed, saying I should run. But I didn't run away. I ran to her. I don't know from where she got her strength, but she threw herself at me, shielding me as my father poured another dose of acid over our bodies. When he was satisfied that he had poured out the last of it, he left. And I've never seen him since."

Beauty took Jeffrey's hand and placed it on her scar. "For a very long time I've felt rejected, unloved and like an outcast, because I believed that if my father could do that to me, to my mother, then who could ever love me?" Tears ran down her cheeks. Jeffrey held onto her and let her cry. When she was done, she looked up at him.

"I'd like to thank you, Jeffrey, because you have helped me to see that there is a life for me and that I don't have to live it alone." She gave him a small smile. "Thank you."

"You're welcome," he said, brushing away her tears.

"Now let's go and find that boy. I think I've cried enough for one day."

"Why did your father do what he did?" Jeffrey asked, not moving to start the car.

"I don't know." Beauty shook her hear. She had never understood. All she knew was that he hated her and her mother. There was no other explanation for what he'd done.

"He just came in the house and burnt you and your mother without a reason?" Jeffrey was shocked.

"He was always a heavy drinker and he had such a temper. But he could always control himself. I thought. I guess he just snapped that day."

"God. Were your parents happy together?" he asked, still not moving.

"As far as I knew."

"So he just turned on you? No wonder you don't trust anyone."

"Maybe he got a better offer somewhere. Who knows?"

"No, he was a coward," Jeffrey said, "I'm glad you told me, but can we talk about it more after we find Njabulo?" Beauty nodded. They went on with their search, stopping to ask people along the way if they had seen the young boy, but still there was no sign of Njabulo.

"What do you think we should do?" Jeffrey asked, turning to Beauty. "We've reached another zone, and we've already passed three of them."

"Maybe we should turn back. Ama must be getting worried by now," Beauty said, even though she wasn't happy that they hadn't found him. Only God knew what might have happened to a child out here in the dark. They turned back to Pamela's house. The number of cars at the front gate had reduced to one, and Ama's car was gone. Where had she gone?

"Where is my sister?" Jeffrey voiced her silent question. He took out his cellphone, and Beauty left him inside the car to make his call. She went inside the house to find the last of the police still busy collecting evidence.

"Did they find him?" she asked one of them, already knowing the answer.

"No," he answered. Beauty nodded, retracing her steps outside. As she walked she vaguely remembered having brought her bag. Where had she dropped it? She couldn't remember. If the police found it she'd definitely go to jail. As she was about to turn back to the house, Jeffrey came to her.

"Ama says she's at Bara. Pamela is still alive. And she also said that you mustn't worry about your bag – she has it."

Beauty covered her face as tears of relief filled her eyes. Happiness flooded. Pamela was still alive!

"Thank you," Beauty said, a weight lifted from her shoulders. "Do you want to go to the hospital? I'll drive you."

"No, could you take me home, please. I left my mother alone. Mandla was there earlier and he scared her. I want to make sure she's alright. I'll go to the hospital tomorrow."

"Okay," Jeffrey said, opening the door for her.

In the car Beauty sat waiting for Jeffrey to start the car and drive away from Pamela's house and its horror. She could already see herself walking into her house and falling asleep, but Jeffrey didn't start the car. Instead he turned towards her, looking at her for a long while.

"I know this is not the right time, but do you think maybe you and I could start from scratch, see where this thing takes us?" Jeffrey asked awkwardly. Beauty looked at him, surprised. She hadn't dared to hope he still wanted her. But here he was asking her.

"Okay," she said with a smile.

"Thank you," he said, leaning over to kiss her before starting the car and driving off.

Chapter 22

Pamela woke up to a splitting headache. Her swollen eyes would open only slightly. Through her half-closed eyelids she took in the ward. This was a familiar place. She'd been here so many times and knew every corner of the place. But this time was different. The pain of her injuries was so severe that she wished she was dead, not alive and having to face her shambles of a life. Beside her, Pamela caught a movement. She tried to turn towards whoever was there. Her muscles screeched at the motion, and she moaned in pain.

"Pamela, don't try to move," Ama said, moving into Pamela's view. She tried to dispel the horror she knew would be reflected in her eyes. She knew she looked bad. Mandla had outdone himself this time. It was a miracle she wasn't dead.

Ama moved forward to prop Pamela up. Pamela noticed Ama's uniform. So she was at work, Pamela thought. It must be Monday then.

"There now," Ama said giving Pamela some water before leaving the room. Probably to check on other patients, Pamela thought.

Now everything that had happened the previous night flashed into her mind. Mandla had unleashed hell the minute they'd stepped into the house, right in front of the kids. Njabulo had screamed, trying to protect her. And then Mandla had turned on him.

She shouldn't have gone back. She should have stuck to the plan and not tried to resuscitate something that was already dead.

"Hello, Pam." It was Beauty.

"Hi," she said, her voice sounding like a croak even to her own ears.

She tried to clear her throat, but there was something unmovable settled there, and she gave up.

"I'm glad to see you're okay," Beauty said, moving forward. Pamela nodded, averting her eyes.

"Did they tell you that Mandla is dead?" Beauty said.

"No." Her swollen eyelids opened very slightly. "I didn't know!"

"When we got there it was already done."

"Who?"

Beauty did not answer.

A strangled sound sounded in Pamela's throat. "Sizwe?"

"Beauty, what are you doing? You're not supposed to upset her!" Ama rushed to them "Now look what you've done. We're going to have to subdue her."

The room spun, and the last thing Pamela could recall was Ama standing over her with a syringe.

Ama tried to stay calm at the sight of her friend thrashing about on the bed, foam bubbling at her mouth. She looked ready to die.

"Go Beauty, wait outside," Ama said, grabbing hold of Pamela's arm.

Finally having got her sedated, she went outside to join Beauty.

"Was that necessary?" she Ama asked. "Has that woman not been through enough?"

"Yes, she has. And we both know that's something she could have avoided."

"You think she deserves this?" Ama asked in disbelief.

"No, Ama. But she needs to know that her decisions put her children in danger."

"Like you were?"

"Yes, something like that."

"She's lying in there, Beauty, her bones broken and her body bruised. Isn't that punishment enough?"

"No." Beauty looked dead serious. "Where are the kids?"

"At my house, Lazaro is with them. They're fine. They'll get through this."

"They have to. They don't have a choice. I just hope they find their brother," Beauty said, her voice showing the sympathy she hadn't shown Pamela.

"Me too."

"Pamela will be fine though, right?" Beauty asked.

"Yes, she doesn't have a choice, either. She has three boys who need her strength."

Yes, she would need all the strength she could find, Ama thought, the strength Mandla had robbed her of for so many years. Maybe now that he was gone, she would find it. And with Beauty and her help, she would make it. Together, they would all make it. Hopefully.

Epilogue

Beauty moved around in the house, checking that everything was in the right place and meticulously clean. She hoped that Pamela would like the changes that Sipho had made. The house looked like new. Beauty was glad about that, because in many ways the house needed to be cleansed, released from what had happened there in the past. It had been a month of scraping paint, knocking down and building walls, and she hoped more than anything that Pamela would be happy.

Beauty waited anxiously in the sitting room. Ama had gone to fetch Pamela from the hospital. Mandla had been buried without her presence, and Pamela's wounds had healed. But Njabulo was still missing. The police were doing the best they could, they kept saying. Beauty hoped this was true, because who knew where that boy was. She couldn't sleep at night wondering what had happened to him.

There was a light knock at the door and Jeffrey entered carrying a night bag. Automatically, Beauty beamed at him. Everything was going well between them, and she was happy. Her mother was pleased with herself, because she had seen it from the beginning, as she kept reminding Beauty. It had been difficult for Beauty, her mother meeting Jeffrey, but it had gone better than expected.

Jeffrey smiled back.

"Where is Pamela?"

"She's coming," Jeffrey said, coming closer to kiss her. "The house looks beautiful, by the way." He kissed her on her forehead.

Sizwe and Sihle walked in. Through their eyes, Beauty could see that they appreciated the changes. Sizwe had lived down the horror of a month ago. He was engaging more with his family, and he and his mother seem to have formed a bond that grew each day.

Pamela slowly walked into the house, Ama and Lazaro walked closely behind her. There was silence as Pamela took stock of the transformation.

"Do you like it, Pam?" Ama asked.

"I love it," she said, smiling over her tears. "Thank you." She turned to look at each of her friends. Ama moved closer to Lazaro, wrapping her arm around his waist.

"Let's eat, everyone," Beauty said, smiling at Ama and Lazaro. Maybe something good would come of that. Beauty looked around her. It was a start, she thought. After everything they had lost, they were all being given another chance.

Other fiction titles published by Modjaji Books

Bom Boy by Yewande Omotoso
Shooting Snakes by Maren Bodenstein
Running & other stories by Makhosazana Xaba
Love Interrupted by Reneilwe Malatji
Team Trinity by Fiona Snyckers
One Green Bottle by Debrah Nixon
got.no.secrets by Danila Botha
Snake by Tracey Farren
The Thin Line by Arja Salafranca
This Place I Call Home by Meg Vandermerwe
The Bed Book of Short Stories edited by Joanne Hichens
    and Lauri Kubuitsile
Whiplash by Tracey Farren